LIMITERS

CHRISTOPHER STODDARD

ITNA
PRESS

Christopher Stoddard © copyright 2014
All rights reserved.
ISBN: 978-0-9912196-1-2
Library of Congress Control Number: 2013954362
Printed in the United States of America.

Cover font: Billy Argel © 2014

I T N A
P R E S S

For B between C and D.

Many thanks and mad love to Gio Black Peter,
Neil Young, Tyler Stone, Christina Whalen,
Caroline Turner, and above all, my mother.

PART ONE:
FAMILY RAVE

Oh! I depend on you as on my mother;
you've always been like a brother to me…
I love you like a brother, I will love you like a father.
– *Arthur Rimbaud to Georges Izambard*

FALL '98

I was in the city last night at this rave called Believe and didn't get home to Connecticut till after six, so I had to sneak inside through the basement doors right below Mom and Sal's bedroom. Sal never sleeps in there anyway, and Mom wasn't home yet. She's fucking Eric, the 19-year-old busboy at Vera's, and probably lied again to Sal that she had to work a double. Sal's an idiot because I've seen her in Eric's beat-up Ford Escort twice this week, but I don't really care that she's cheating on Sal 'cause he's not my father.

Probably right around the time I was dropping another tab of acid at Believe, a nest of flying ants was breaking open somewhere in our basement. By the time I made it home, tripping balls, after all the rat poison in the acid fucked up my stomach and I had to take two dumps in the piss-reeking bathroom on the train, the bugs were everywhere. I found Raid under the sink that I pee in when it's too late to go upstairs, and sprayed and sprayed until every last one of them was dead. I woke up covered in dead ants, with at least a hundred more of them all over my bed and on the concrete floor and Astroturf. They were stuck to the shower curtains that Sal hung around my bedroom area to give me privacy in this damp, moldy shithole—I used to share one of the three real bedrooms upstairs with Max, but I haven't lived up there since he died about two years ago. Now I'm the only one left in the family whose last name is Mason. My real father's locked up, and I don't speak to his side of the family 'cause they're a bunch of assholes.

Feeling sick from inhaling too much Raid, not to mention all the acid I did, I'm running to the sink to vomit just as Mom's coming down the basement stairs with a basket of laundry.

"Kyle! Christ, I just cleaned that sink. You were out drinking again, weren't you!" Clutching the basket so tightly her knuckles are red, she stands there in her tight, faded black jeans, a stained black apron wrapped around her tiny waist, and a white button-down shirt that's too small, and keeps screaming at me. Her wavy brown hair is full and shiny even though she's been working all day, but she smells like cigarettes and meat, which is making me more nauseous. Any guys that have met her—Max's friends or mine, or her co-workers at the diner—all want to fuck her. I guess that's why she gets away with being such a miserable bitch to everybody, but that doesn't work on me. I've read about Oedipus in school, and I'm the furthest thing from him; I don't want to kill my father or fuck my mother, but I hate them both and wish they never had me.

I turn on the faucet, forcing the bile-soaked chunks down the drain with my pointer finger. "Get off my back, okay! I'm not my father so stop treating me like him!"

"Then stop acting like him, druggie boy! And you think I don't know about your sleepovers with Jack?" Dropping the basket on the floor, she points her finger in my face. "You can leave! I won't have that nasty shit in my house."

I turn off the faucet and walk toward my bedroom area. "You should talk. Whore."

"You little cocksucker!" she yelps, smacking me in the back of the head.

"What'd you say to her!" Sal is stomping down the stairs, my younger half-siblings Mark and Theresa following behind him.

Theresa grabs ahold of Sal's arm. "Don't, Dad! Please!"

"Take Mark back upstairs to the living room with Grandpa," he says. His fists are clenched, and he's staring at me unblinkingly. He's wearing greasy navy blue pants and a stained white T-shirt. His arms are jacked from all the manual labor at the silicon factory in Newtown, but his stomach sticks out. I stay put while Mark and Theresa do as they're told. "And you can just get out with that mouth of yours. I'm sick of the way you talk to her."

Mom charges up the stairs. "I can't deal with this shit right now. I have to get back to work."

Sal huffs at me, picks up the basket of clothes and walks to the washer on the other side of the basement.

"You want me gone, I will leave! Don't think I won't."

"Go! What are you waiting for!" she yells from upstairs. "I'm done."

I'm hiding behind the hedges alongside our neighbor's house until Mom heads back to the diner and Sal leaves for work. As each of their cars pulls out of the driveway, the headlights reflect off the windows of the houses across the street, blinding me for a second. Hurrying into the house, I call my friend Bridget. She tells me she's moving back to her dorm tonight, and if I get us a ride in a four-seat car, I can come; her dad only drives a pickup truck. I hang up, then call Jack, Max's best friend. Jack says he can take us, but the transmission in his car died the other day, so we'll have to ride in his brother's hearse. His crazy goth-dressing brother bought it from a funeral home that went out of business. All of Max's friends feel responsible for me, want to do for me what he would've done. But if he were alive I wouldn't be doing this.

While waiting for Jack and Bridget to get here, I rummage through Sal's closet, finding his water jug filled to the brim with singles and change. There's got to be at least a couple hundred bucks. I'm not taking anything else, not even my books. Other than going to raves, reading is pretty much the only thing I love to do. But my junior year of high school just started, and they're making me take English honors classes, so everyone thinks I'm a big dork now. Plus, the books they have us studying are shit. As I walk out, Grandpa grumbles and turns on his hearing aid while Mark and Theresa continue playing Super Nintendo, their eyes glued to the TV.

"Where are you going?" Grandpa asks.

"Just down the street."

He farts and says something else, but I can't make it out because I'm already out the door. Jack honks the horn. With the heavy water jug in my arms, I walk to the car and climb in. Bridget's snoring in the backseat. She must've gotten drunk at home or taken some pills.

"You alright, dude?" Jack asks. I don't reply. We drive off in the rickety hearse, the jug of change bouncing on my lap and making me kind of hard. I think of the times he and I jerked off to porn together and wonder if we'll ever do it again. He starts telling me about some girl he's fucking, but his voice is muffled as I stare at the passenger-side mirror, trying to see my reflection in the dark.

...

Central Connecticut State University could be mistaken for projects if there weren't so many white kids walking around the campus grounds. Bridget's college is in New Britain, a small city that feels almost desolate, with just a few zombies for residents, the school being the only normal part of it, which isn't saying much. She lives in the Quad: four buildings built around a large concrete square where students hang out, and where I've already vomited twice from drinking and once from eating too many shrooms.

Now that she's back in college, she's skinnier than usual; her daily diet is a bowl of raisin bran for breakfast, no lunch, a box of wine for dinner and four or five Xanax for dessert, with the occasional dime bag of coke as a 5 a.m. snack. She only fucks guys who sell drugs or are willing to buy them for her—and everyone at the college knows it. Her hair is naturally brown, but she tried bleaching it blond, and it came out a green-yellow, similar to the color of the dying bamboo plants I've seen in the window of the Chinese restaurant three blocks from the dorms. Most days she lets me use her cafeteria pass, which is nice of her, but besides that she's a bitch. She's failing all her classes and going off on me over nothing whenever we're together.

I try to keep myself busy applying for jobs, eventually getting hired to work as a cashier at Congress Rotisserie on West Main Street. When the bosses are in the back of the restaurant, I sneak forkfuls of stuffing with gravy, yams or mashed potatoes. Whatever I can get in my mouth is what I eat for the whole day. Once in a while I take cash from the register and buy a big dinner to share with Bridget. But the free food and space I've been giving her clearly isn't making a difference 'cause we're in another fight tonight.

The dyke resident assistant kicks open Bridget's door, bat in hand. "Is he hitting you again?!" she screams. She's had a thing for Bridget since the second Bridget started college here. "Time to go!" she says with spittle on her lower lip. She's got her crooked nose in my face, and I smell her rank breath and almost gag. Bridget doesn't say anything; she just sits on the bed, arms crossed, staring coldly at me.

"Well, where am I supposed to go?" I say.

"Oh, you're going! No little bastard is gonna mess with one of my girls on my watch."

"I'm sorry for the noise," Bridget says, "I'll make him leave by the end of the week. I can't just throw him out on the street."

"End of the week, Bridget. I won't have this on my floor. I'll call the cops next time," the dyke promises, her deep voice cracking, suddenly sweet and almost feminine. "Are you sure you're okay, doll?"

Bridget's in class when I move out of the dorm, but the R.A. sees me off, clapping sarcastically as I walk toward the elevator on "her floor."

"We're so sorry to see you go, Mason," she says. "If I ever catch you back here, I'm going to beat the shit out of your wimpy, weak ass, then call the cops."

15

I don't say anything at first. Instead, I give her one of those looks that the tranny who worked at the Burger King drive-through in Milford always gave my mother and me. The tranny was a ginormous black guy with six-inch fingernails that were painted purple and had tiny plastic crystals in the shape of cocks glued to them. If it hadn't been for the nails, I'd have thought she looked like a defensive football player. She was all scrunched up in the window, could barely squeeze our bags of fast food out of it because there was only enough room for her head and shoulders. But I always showed her respect, saying politely from the passenger seat of my mom's Chevette, "Please, may I have some extra ketchup?" and, "Thank you. Have a nice day." She'd look at me with attitude as if I had an ulterior motive, especially given the way Mom would stare. I guess if you're a tranny you have to be distrustful of people. This bitch has no excuse, though, and I can never keep my mouth shut for long when it comes to nasty people like her. The elevator dings, doors slide open.

"By the way. Bridget is straight. You're wasting your time."

She turns beet red and charges down the hall, but the automatic doors close before she can get at me.

...

Donald and Joann are the perfect couple, the kind, generous type that actually deserves to be parents someday. Donald never takes his eyes off Joann, and she's so attentive, always by his side, on the couch holding hands and kissing him, or cooking and cleaning. Jack met them at some rave. After I escaped from Bridget's crazy dorm, they took me in as easily as one would a stray kitten, giving me a place to sleep in their attic. They live on the top floor of a duplex in Manchester, another town in Connecticut, but it doesn't remind me of where I'm from. It's so far north; it's practically Rhode Island. The houses are different, two-family ones seem bigger, older.

There are two other guys living in the attic: Nick, a 23-year-old hippie with longish blond hair, a scruffy beard, pillow lips and blue-green eyes; and an AWOL marine named Ariel who's around the same age as Nick, has a shaved head and is always tripping on LSD. The attic's freezing, so we have to share a portable heater on a rotating schedule; every two days I get it. When it's not my turn, Nick lets me borrow some of his sweaters at night to keep warm. I wear two of the three like normal, and the third I wrap around my head the way my mom does a bathroom towel after she showers.

Joann lent me an old cassette player to listen to music before bed. Sometimes it just shuts off because it's too cold. She has a lot of tapes by Hole. I like the words to the songs. I've never listened to music like it before. At school everyone's into rap and hip-hop.

17

Donald sells ecstasy at parties, but he also works at a hardware store in the center of town. He stays up almost every night smoking glass and spinning records in the living room while we dance and roll and trip, talking about plans for the future. After Donald goes to work and Joann passes out, and Ariel's busy date-raping some half-conscious chick in the attic, Nick and I will eat whatever food is in the fridge. There's usually just stale crinkle fries or a few leftover bowls of Top Ramen in there, but we make the most of it. Nick's already showed me the ropes, how rotten food can taste good when the only thing left to eat is your stomach.

I'm sucking juice out of a can of clams; Joann and Donald don't have an opener, so I have to use a dull pair of scissors to puncture holes in it. Luckily, I'm still able to pull out a few chunks of meat. Nick's forcing rock-hard, two-week-old pasta down his throat. It's silent in the apartment except for my slurping and his crunching. Ariel's passed out in the attic, Donald's at work, and Joann's not feeling well so she's been in her room all day. Nick tosses the crusty paper plate of Ragu and ziti into the garbage, along with the slimy can he's snatched from my lips.

"Put on my backpack, little buddy. We're going grocery shopping."

I'm excited but also nervous because I know what he means; we've done it at least four or fives times since I've been here. He runs up to the attic and drags Ariel out of bed. Ariel's the decoy. We can always count on him to do something in public that causes a scene; while everyone's focused on getting him out of the store, Nick fills the backpack as if he were an elf packing Santa's sack of gifts, slipping in a pint of milk, a couple boxes of mac and cheese, butter, ramen, fruit rollups, pre-packaged deli meats, bagels, a box of cereal if it fits. If not, then ice cream and maybe some oranges. Sometimes we'll be in a rush, get paranoid about getting caught, so Nick will just start grabbing whatever's on the nearest shelves. Last time it was four cans of clams, a couple jars of grape jelly and the pasta sauce.

Ariel's eyes are half closed as we make our way to the grocery store, and he ends up walking into a tree. Laughing hysterically, we help him to his feet, Nick slapping him to keep him awake. He really should be home sleeping after the four-night party he's just gotten home from, but we need him here if we're going to do this.

To get to the center of town, we have to walk up a steep street, and only after we reach the top do we see the fluorescent-lit treasure-trove filled with edible goodness. We run down the hill into the bustling town, "bustling" in Manchester meaning there are three or four people on the street other than us. Before the grocery store, there's a long line of little buildings that house the other shops in town: Manchester Hardware, Sally's Beauty Supply, Pet Surplus, Needling a Haystack Tailors and Diner. That's what the diner says out front, just "Diner," not Manchester Diner or Frankie's Diner or whatever. But to us, it's a five-star establishment. We eye the people inside as they shovel tuna melts and cheeseburgers into their faces, little kids licking the maple syrup dripping from the corners of their pancake-stuffed mouths. The families eating look back at us as if we were dogs begging for food. The door to the restaurant swings open, and a fat pretty woman with big dyed-red hair, wearing a nametag that says "Annie," rolls outside.

"Can I help you boys?" she says. "Either eat here or Tony's at the end of Main. It's Christmas, you know, nothing else's open. But stop staring in my window like a bunch of animals."

Ariel laughs out loud—I didn't know he was even aware of his surroundings. I'm about to smile and say, "Thanks but no thanks," when Nick jumps in front of us.

"You've twisted our arms, Annie," he says. "And Merry Christmas."

Smiling, she moves aside, and we file into the toasty warm restaurant that smells like apple pie, melted cheese and coffee. Seating us in a booth in the corner, she slaps three greasy menus on the table in front of us, the covers revealing the full name of the place: Annie's Diner.

"You own this?" I ask uneasily.

"Three generations," she says shivering, her nipples hard beneath a thin white blouse with ketchup stains on it. "Man, is it cold out! Start with coffee?"

"Sure," I say, except I don't really drink coffee, but when I'm starving, everything sounds good. Filling my cup halfway with sugar and so much milk it overflows onto the table, I sop it up with the complimentary bread and butter. I order a ham-egg-and-cheese sandwich with a side of French fries, French toast and a black-and-white milkshake.

"The best shakes in Connecticut!" Annie boasts.

Nick asks, "Can I have a double-chili-cheeseburger with

raw onions, a side of bacon and linguini Alfredo?" We all look to Ariel to place his order, but he's fallen asleep sitting up. "Long day of traveling," Nick explains, "Why don't we get a tuna melt and fries for him, okay?"

"You got it boys," Annie says while walking away.

The last of the other customers leave: a fat mother and her two whiny boys. Now it's just Annie and us. I'm eating so slowly, savoring each bite, every minute—every second— before she gives us the bill. It's my first big meal in months; Thanksgiving came and went without me noticing. When we're finished, she hands us the check, telling us to take our time, she's knocked off the charges for the coffee and the milkshake.

"Miguel! Shut it down!" she yells, turning the sign around on the front door. "Be right back, boys."

"Take your time," Nick says.

As soon as her fat silhouette disappears down the narrow hallway leading to the kitchen, Nick hops to his feet, a couple ketchup-dipped French fries in his fingers. He grabs Ariel by the collar of his shirt. Ariel's surprisingly coherent, probably from the food. Feeling really guilty, I'm the last to follow. She's been so warm to us, feeding us and giving us a deal on the bill, and in return, we're basically robbing her. We shouldn't have come here. I'd have felt better stealing from the grocery store. The grocery store isn't a person. There's no face on the can of clams back at the apartment, but there is one on the milkshake in my stomach: Annie.

The bell jingles when Nick opens the front door, and I

realize too late how slowly I've been following. Annie grabs me by the back of my dirty white T-shirt, slamming me to the floor. We make eye contact, and I can tell how disappointed she is in me.

"You fucking kids! Miguel! Call the cops! We've got dine-and-ditchers! You sons of bitches!"

Running over, Nick tackles her to the ground. She falls like a cow that's been tipped. The thump's loud but not as disturbing as the sound of Ariel kicking her in the ribs with his USMC-issued combat boots, a blank look on his face. I don't tell him to stop. I don't do anything, but Nick eventually pulls him back. Ariel's panting and drooling like a rabid dog.

"Kyle, get the fuck up," Nick says sternly like someone's dad. Miguel hasn't come out of the kitchen, but I hear sirens in the distance, so he must've called the cops. Annie moans, rolling around on the floor, finally settling in the fetal position. An image of my mom goes through my head. "Now dude!" Nick yells, wide-eyed.

Rising to my feet, I snap out of it and run away with them. Halfway home I burp. Tasting the milkshake, I realize the guilt I feel will upset me so much that all the food will go right through me, my body not absorbing any of the nutrients from it. I'll just have diarrhea when I get back to the apartment, and within a couple more hours, I'll be starving again.

...

It's the morning after a rave called Dream at the Municipal Cafe in Hartford. At the party I smoked a PCP cigarette with this gay guy Wesley, a well-known party promoter who's always hitting on me. One second I'm dancing, the next taking a drag, and now I'm staring at myself in the bathroom mirror back at Donald and Joann's.

There's an insane after-party going on; I hear Wes cackling in the living room, the bass from the music hammering the walls, the neighbor on the first floor banging on the ceiling, but I stay in the bathroom, keep right on staring at myself in the mirror, noticing I'm wearing some fat dude's extra-extra-large gray T-shirt doused in sweat and smelling of rank body odor—not mine—an orange Nike logo on the front of it, thinking maybe I did acid at the party, but then remembering that I smoked the angel dust.

I have the makings of a mustache, but it hasn't fully grown in yet. Sometimes I shave, but I usually don't bother because it makes no difference; I'm ugly either way. My Caffeine hoodie is nowhere to be found, but I still have on the dark blue Adidas visor I stole from Bridget when she kicked me out.

Nick busts open the bathroom door without knocking, whining that he has to piss. "Dude, you look crazy!" he says through a thick chuckle.

I check my reflection in the mirror again, then turn back to Nick, erupting into laughter. He's pissing on the seat. As I tell him what happened, how the dust I smoked warped time, I get a look at his long, thick dick without him noticing. He zips up and doesn't wash his hands. His eyes are half closed and he's wasted from whatever he's been doing all night.

"Little bro, you've gotta come with us to Cali," he says, smoothing his hair behind his ears. "You're like family now. Plus, I need you to keep me company and make me laugh whenever Ariel disappears. What do you think?"

A couple days ago Nick showed Ariel and me the bus ticket he bought, telling us about his plans to move to San Diego and start fresh. He said it's always sunny in California, not freezing and snowy like Connecticut. Ariel is coming too. They're going to find jobs there, but until they do, they'll just panhandle and sleep on the beach. Nick says everyone's really happy on the West Coast, so it's easy to beg for money there.

"Hell yeah I wanna go!" Smiling widely, I feel how I did on the rare occasions when Max invited me out with him and his friends.

...

Now that I've been living with Donald and Joann for a couple months, I know who they really are. The first time I heard Joann's muffled cries was when Donald was quietly beating the shit out of her before he left for work at six in the morning because his cup of coffee wasn't hot enough.

This morning I'm sitting up in bed, listening to him hurting her again. Whenever I don't have the heater, the coldness and their fighting keeps me from sleeping. Ariel always has it after me, and he's sound asleep right now, oblivious. Nick's up too, but as usual he's not doing anything.

"Mind your own business and go back to sleep," he says, knowing I'm awake and worried.

After hearing Donald leave for work, I say, "I'm just gonna run down to check on her." I always think of my mother and real father, how he abused her when Max and I were babies. I don't remember any of it, but Max did, and I feel now how I did when he told me about it.

"Not now, dude," Nick says, stopping me at the door. "Wait a little while."

Fifteen minutes later, he agrees to come down with me.

"Hi Joann," I say groggily as we walk into the kitchen.

"Hi!" she says in her chipper voice. "How about some breakfast burritos?"

Nick doesn't say anything as he lights a smoke and sits at the dirty kitchen table. Joann's hands are shaking when she pulls the food out the freezer, so I offer to set the table. While

25

putting down paper plates, I examine her with my eyes, noticing she has no visible injuries—Donald always hits her below the neck, and she never wears low-cut blouses or short skirts. She pops the burritos in the microwave, then goes to her room to sob quietly, but we can still hear her.

The front she puts on is pretty ridiculous, with her prettied-up ugly face and raggedy housewife dresses, as if she's fooling any of us. She always tries curling her straight brown hair for Donald, but it just comes out wavy and dry, and she has high cheekbones, but they're more like pointy nipples rather than like cheekbones that accentuate the face of a gorgeous model. She's the cook of our "family," but hardly ever eats. On many mornings, I've heard Donald telling her she's fat, so she's constantly making herself throw up—you can hear everything in that attic—and her breath always stinks. She's just so helpless. My pity for her is slowly turning into resentment and hatred. Or maybe I'm just exhausted.

...

Nick's been seeing this new girl Tiffany. She's beautiful, and a hippie like him: straight black hair down to her butt, thin body, big lips and long dresses she wears all the time with this cool wool coat she knitted herself. It's bright orange, makes me think of Florida whenever I'm around her. Last night we all snorted heroin and got drunk, and she was crocheting a forest green blanket with specks of yellow that reminded me of birds in trees. I had a really high fever the last couple days that just started going down, and I'm thinking the dope and alcohol may have helped kill some of the germs, which is a relief because I've been too scared to go to the doctor in case they want to speak to my parents.

Other than me being sick, it's a usual weekday morning after one of Donald's after-parties. He was so wasted earlier he puked all over the kitchen and went to bed. Joann didn't follow; she was—and still is—too drunk to obey the rules. The cracked-out ravers are trickling out slowly, melting away like snow in springtime, till eventually they've all gone. Ariel hasn't headed upstairs yet because he's too high and there aren't any chicks around. Nick's just gone up with Tiffany, so now it's just Ariel, Joann and I.

Ariel and Joann are playing Celebrity, just the two of them—the game is pointless without at least six players. But they're having a blast: he's on shrooms and she's laughing hysterically, especially when he tries impersonating The Notorious B.I.G. because it's so opposite from his normal appearance; he usually looks like the poster boy for the Aryan Nations. Finding black shoe polish under the kitchen sink, he takes it into the bathroom and starts smearing it all over his face and arms.

"I'm having, like, an out-of-body experience right now guys," he says, reentering the living room, "Like I'm someone else."

Grabbing a pillow on the couch and shoving it underneath the T-shirt he's wearing, his costume is now complete. He's a fat black celebrity, and only I get it 'cause I'm the one who wrote "B.I.G." on a piece of paper and dropped it in the bowl they're using to play the game. But he's making Joann laugh so hard, and it's real, makes me think of how Sal made Mom laugh sometimes.

The afternoon's come, and it's like Donald doesn't exist at all, let alone him being in the next room sleeping. But from out of nowhere he barges into the living room, and seeing how closely Joann's sitting next to Ariel with a smile on her sad, emaciated face, he clenches a fist and knocks her front teeth out.

"You fucking whore!"

Ariel bolts wearing the B.I.G. stuff. He runs out of the house so quickly it's like Roadrunner leaving Coyote in a cloud of dust. Compared with how violent he was with Annie, he's like the complete opposite of himself in this situation. This is the first time Donald's hit Joann in front of us, and to my knowledge, the first time he's punched her in the face. The front teeth just came off the gums. I bet that doesn't happen to most people who've been punched just once. A bloody lip, a cut in the mouth, *maybe* a chipped tooth, but Joann getting her teeth knocked out from a single punch proves they weren't held in too tightly in the first place. Come to think of it, she never eats dairy. The closest thing to milk she ever drinks is the come Donald makes her swallow every morning.

She has her hand over mouth, trying to stop the blood pouring out of it because she doesn't want to make a mess on the stained couch and gummed-up carpet. He'll be really pissed at her if she does. By the worried look in her glassy eyes, it's pretty obvious that's what's running through her weak mind. It all makes more sense to me now, the way my real father abused my mother, the way she treated Max and me when we were younger, why Sal would beat us for spilling milk or swearing. It's all about control.

God, I'm so angry with everyone! The game of Celebrity is over, and Joann hasn't figured out Ariel's costume. Donald goes after her again. I pick up one of his turntables and chuck it in his path, but he sees me in his periphery and ducks, which is surprising considering he isn't wearing his glasses. He always looks like a bookworm: big eyeglasses, stringy neck and bald pea head. But now he's more like a red earthworm with Tourette's.

"After all I've done for you, you little shit! You come into my house and throw shit at me when I'm having words with my bitch!" he screams, punching me in the face, then wrapping his grimy hands around my neck and slamming me against the bloodstained living room wall. "I could kill you!" His eyes are bloodshot and drilling into mine like a jackhammer. The yellow rays shining through the filthy windows, the wrecked room, it's all turning white. Maybe he'll stop the blood pumping into my brain long enough for me to pass out and never wake up.

Nick comes out of nowhere and rips Donald off me like a Band-Aid. I feel a rush of blood to my head, the color in everything returning quickly: golden sunlight, browning white walls, Joann's red mouth and gray skin, Nick's long blond hair. He doesn't resemble Max at all; Max had dark hair, a short crew cut, was wide and muscular but nowhere near as tall as Nick. Though he might've grown to Nick's height if he had had the chance to become a man. I shake the thought from my head as I recover from the attack.

Tiffany runs in while Donald and Nick push and punch each other. They tumble down the front stairs. Nick jumps to his feet first, gets his arms around Donald's waist and tosses him outside in the snow.

"Cool the fuck down, bro!" Nick says, panting. "You're going to beat on your girlfriend and now a sixteen-year-old? What the hell is wrong with you?"

I follow them outside, standing on the porch behind Nick. Tiffany is alongside me, her hand on my bony shoulder. Donald's just lying there facedown in the snow, not moving. I hear police sirens. One of the neighbors must've called the cops. Nick turns to Tiffany and me. He looks a little banged up, but has no serious wounds.

"C'mon, let's go check on her," she whispers, taking my hand, "Nick'll stay here with Donald and wait for the cops."

As we start for the stairs, I look back at Nick. Donald's on his feet and has a brick in his hand—a piece from the chimney that's been falling apart for as long as I've been living here.

"No!" I shout, but it's too late. He pounds Nick in the head. Nick makes a weird moaning sound as he falls backward off the porch into a pile of snow.

The blood, the fucking blood melting the snow, Tiffany screaming for help, the cops pulling up, Joann gurgling something from the window upstairs, I just stand silently. The medics arrive, carry an unconscious Nick into an ambulance, while Tiffany lies to the cops, telling them I'm her younger brother and she's looking after me till our dad comes back from a business trip. They take Donald away in handcuffs, spitting and mouthing off to them. Joann comes out to argue with the EMTs, insisting she's fine, she'll get her face looked at another time, she has to stay home and clean up because her husband will be back soon.

After I grab a few of my things and steal some of Donald's drug money in the bathroom—I saw him hiding it in the toilet once—Tiffany walks me back to her place. As we walk, I listen to her whimpering for Nick, the way the sound forms a melody with the wheezing wind and melting icicles dripping off the roofs of the houses we pass. I'm not high anymore, but I feel weird, so I guess I'm shaken up and still pretty sick. We don't say much to each other as she lets me into the apartment, telling me to rest, she'll be back later, she has to go be with Nick. I hope he doesn't die like Max.

...

I look at myself in the mirror. The hot shower fogged it up, so my face is unclear. I wonder if the bruise has faded at all, but I don't expect much change because the fight was less than two days ago. I just had to get involved, mind other people's business, didn't I? And now the mirror clears, and there I am: fucked-up face, and homeless yet again.

Tiffany is letting me stay at her place for the next week or so until her father gets home from a business trip, and then I'm off to San Diego with Ariel—and hopefully Nick, but I don't know for sure at this point. He's still in the hospital and it's my fault. There was so much blood on him and in a dark red puddle seeping into the snow like cherry syrup on a snow cone.

I smell incense, weed and cheese coming through the bathroom door, hear the Beatles song "A Day in the Life" playing from a record in the living room. Tiffany's making us mushroom-and-grilled-cheese sandwiches for lunch, the kind she sold that time in the parking lot outside the Phish concert so we could all buy mescaline. Ariel got so high he stripped naked, then ran off searching for the closest church, but the cops got him before he could be saved. Mistaking the cops for demons, he punched two of them in the face before two more came, held him down on the sidewalk and kicked the shit out of him. An ambulance showed up, EMTs sedated him and took him to the hospital. The cops waited outside his room, but hadn't handcuffed him, so he escaped through the window, running barefoot in the snow all the way back to Donald and Joann's, wearing nothing but a hospital gown.

A wad of bills drops out the back pocket of my wide-legged JNCOs as I put them back on. It's about 80 bucks. I'd have never stolen from Donald when I thought of him and Joann as the perfect couple, but everything's ruined now.

"Thank you for the sandwich, the shower, washing my shit...everything," I say to Tiffany, walking into the living room.

"Good news!" she says while handing me a joint and my sandwich. "I just got off the phone with Ariel. Nick's concussion isn't as bad as they thought. He's going to be okay and should be out tomorrow."

"That's awesome! That makes me feel a million times better. I definitely need to go buy my bus ticket first thing tomorrow." The song by the Beatles ends, I bite into my sandwich, and Tiffany sets down the blanket she's making. She takes a hit of a new joint and passes it to me.

"Ariel's gonna stay at the hospital with Nick till he gets out. They'll be over in the morning," she says, giving me a disapproving look. "Listen, have you called to check on your mother?"

"My mother! Why would you say that? What does she have to do with anything?"

She exhales deeply. "She's your *mother*, Kyle. And Nick and Ariel are adults. They're like ten years older than you. Are you sure you want to go so far away from home?"

"What do you mean? This is my home. You guys are."

"They can't take care of you." She doesn't say it to be

mean, I know this. But it's possible she's just giving me a hard time because she can't come with us; her father's making her go back to college for the spring semester. Anyway, it doesn't really matter what she thinks because Nick's the one who invited me, so I'm not listening to her, but I'm grateful for her friendly concern.

She passes the joint again. Puffing on it, I lie on my back on the clean carpeting, my head resting on a pillow with the cover she knitted from white yarn. I feel like I'm dirtying it up even though I just showered. The weed takes effect, the ceiling droops, my eyes get heavy, and I fall asleep.

Morning comes more quickly than I want it to, the doorbell ringing and someone knocking on the window waking me up. "Open the goddamn door, baby!" Nick yells from outside.

I hear Tiffany coming out of the bedroom, the bottom of her long thick skirt making swishy sounds like a broom as she glides across the hardwood floor in the hallway and the linoleum in the kitchen. Opening the front door, she invites a bandaged Nick and loopy-eyed Ariel inside. Groggy, I stand up and walk into the kitchen. Nick has a black eye and a bandage on his head. He kisses Tiffany on the lips, and she kisses his wounds. Ariel slaps my back with one hand while wiping the sweat off his face with the other—he must be detoxing.

"Sup, Kyle!" he says. Ignoring him for a second, I extend a hand to Nick, who just grabs me by the arm and pulls me toward him, giving me a big hug and tousling my hair with his scabby knuckles.

"What time does the bus leave tomorrow? I've got my own cash for my ticket now," I say.

"Cool," Nick says, "Go grab your shit, little buddy."

Hurrying into the living room, I pack the visor, a couple T-shirts and the Hole tape. When I come back, Tiffany is sitting at the kitchen table, calling us a cab, looking sad. Nick is standing behind her, smoothing her dark straight hair with his swollen hands. We all hear Ariel taking a massive dump in the bathroom and start laughing as we hold our noses.

Before we know it, the cab is outside, Tiffany is crying, and Nick is trying to kiss her goodbye. He whispers something in her ear; she nods her head and looks at me. It's as if she's seeing me off to college. I'm her son who just graduated high school, and she's sad I'm leaving the nest, but at the same time proud because it's the next step toward a bright future for me. I know it's the right thing too. San Diego, here I come!

The Peter Pan Bus station in Hartford is crowded at 6 a.m. on a Tuesday. The men in suits waiting to take the buses to work in Manhattan are mostly to blame. What a long three-hour commute they have. The snow is melting, sliding off the roofs of the buses, splattering on the ground like water balloons, and I imagine what our bus will look like once we're farther south. In Mississippi, the dried dirt left over from the muddy slush on the wheels of the bus will be washed away by sporadic rainstorms, and when we drive through the deserts in Arizona, the scorching sun will lighten the signature green color in the Peter Pan logo on the roof. Ariel will sleep the whole way there because he'll be out of drugs and detoxing while Nick and I have intense conversations about our lives.

"Hand over your bus money, dude," Nick says, smacking the back of my head, "I'll go in and get your ticket. You probably have to be over eighteen anyway."

"Thanks," I say, giving him cash and sitting back on the bench where Ariel is going to town on his fingernails.

"Chill the fuck out, man," Nick says, grabbing Ariel's arm. "Walk inside with me."

Sometimes I think Ariel is mentally retarded. I wonder if it's because of all the acid he's done, or a genetic defect, or some traumatic experience he had while in the Marine Corps. He never did explain why he went AWOL. Then again, girls think he's really hot and like his simplemindedness, so maybe it's all an act.

Looking to my left, I see a bus with "San Diego" lit up in white letters above the windshield pulling out the lot. Shit, we've missed our bus! Hiding my duffle bag under the bench, I run inside, pushing past the last of the businessmen. "Nick! Guys! The bus just left!"

I make my way to the counter, but neither of my friends is in sight. No one is, really. It's after six now. The crowds of people have left the building and boarded the buses that are driving out the parking lot in droves. An employee shows up at the counter, yawning while pinning a nametag to the chest pocket of her uniform.

"Excuse me," I say, my tone panicky like the voice of a boy who got lost in the mall, "Have you seen my friends? One has long blond hair, the other cut really short?"

She reaches for a white envelope on the counter and hands it to me. "You must be Kyle. They said you'd be here in a couple of minutes. This is for you."

Heart pounding, breath shortening, I rip open the envelope, finding my ticket and change in it. But it's not a ticket to San Diego; it's one to Bridgeport. Written in all caps on the inside of the envelope, it says, "Time to go home, kid! We love you!"

"No, no, no!"

"Are you okay? Do you want me to call someone?"

"Leave me alone!" I don't have a family. Dragging my feet, I walk out the station and onto Spruce Street, make a left on Asylum Street and head downtown.

...

Max was lying awkwardly against a dirty curb as his life pooled in a pothole a couple feet away. The Los Angeles Raiders logo on the back of the bloody Starter jacket covering him could've been engraved on the front of a tombstone for a swashbuckling pirate. I had the Miami Dolphins version of the jacket, which was bright orange and dark sea green, neither of which went well with red. I never wanted the fucking thing. I didn't give a shit about football or those nylon and polyester death traps.

They cost over a hundred bucks each. Mom had spent a good chunk of change on them for Christmas. Max and I knew what we were getting, by sneaking into the attic, carefully unwrapping our presents, inspecting the goods, then taping them back up without her noticing. We'd been going up there every Christmas for two or three years. Sure, it ruined the element of surprise, but at least we always found out sooner whether or not we'd be getting what we really wanted.

And I didn't want the jacket. I just wanted to look good like Max. He'd always been concerned with his looks, religiously changing his clothes five to ten times before going out. We both had pale skin, but my hair is dirty blond, and his was black; I'm skinny, and he was muscular—thoughts of our looks popped into my head that afternoon he died in front me, while I tried to remember if I'd kept any of the Polaroid pictures he'd been having me take of him. He always said a mirror couldn't show you how you truly look to someone else. It'd only been a week since he sat on the lower level of our bunk beds, staring with an exaggerated toughness at me, the cam-

era. I wanted to recall his clothing in better detail, which brightly colored T-shirt and jeans he'd mixed and matched to put together whatever outfit he'd planned on wearing that night. I couldn't. But I was able to picture his eyes, how they'd seemed to be begging the lens for a sign of approval.

"Max! Please, God!" I said, nothing changing.

"I called the police!" shouted a deep voice from a nearby house. The deep voice was too scared to come outside and help, but there was nothing to be afraid of anymore; the gang had already left. They'd taken Max's life but not what they wanted—his jacket was still there. And I was wearing mine, and it was too big! It was too fucking big, and I hadn't wanted to tell Mom that because she'd been so proud of herself for finding them on sale—she's obsessed with couponing. Maybe if I had, that day wouldn't have happened. I'd have been at the store trying on a smaller size while Max sifted through the clothes racks to see if there was anything else he wanted. Mom would've been annoyed, but that'd have been nothing compared to how she felt when the police told her that her eldest son had been killed.

All those Sundays she made us go to church—Our Fucking Fathers and Hail the Slut Mary's—God still did it to us. He should've warned us about the four-door Mustang with tinted windows. He should've saved Max from the wiggers who jumped him. Max told me to run as soon as he saw the car—he must've recognized it from somewhere—but I just hid behind some bushes in front of a neighbor's house. They all hopped out, one of them pointing a gun in Max's face, the rest punching him in the head and kicking him in the ribs over and over. But God didn't care. He didn't shield Max from the nervous one who accidentally pulled the trigger of the gun he had aimed at Max's neck.

"Yo what the fuck!" said the driver. They all got back in the car and sped away, leaving behind the shooter who stood frozen as Max gurgled and bled to death at his feet. Snapping out of it, the shooter ran off.

"I called the police!" shouted that deep voice, as if to make me feel better or safer. I felt nothing.

WINTER

Wesley lives two blocks from the Municipal Cafe in a loft that reminds me of one I partied at in Manhattan on Halloween last year, after this rave called Boo. He's in his mid-30s, tall, stringy and has light brown hair that's buzzed on the sides and spiky on top. He said if I ever needed a place to crash I could always stay with him—I told him about Donald and Joann's fucked-up relationship one time when we were all rolling. But I never considered taking him up on his offer till now because he's always giving me faggy looks.

Sniffling from the cold morning walk, I ring the buzzer to his apartment. It's only a little after seven in the morning, so he's either just gotten home from a rave or getting ready for work. When I reach his floor, he's waiting by the elevator with open arms.

"Oh, you poor baby! C'mon in." He pulls me close, rubbing my back. "I am so sorry. Nick and Ariel are good guys but completely unreliable. You came to the right place, Kylie. Yes, you did," he says, leading me into the apartment. House music plays at low volume from a boom box in the kitchen. Snatching a bottle of L.A. Looks gel from the bathroom, he goops it onto his hair.

"Take a seat, baby. There's cereal." He picks up a can of

hairspray and spritzes his hair until it's as stiff as the dead insects in my old bedroom. "There's a New Year's Eve party at Muni toniiight," he sings. "It's called Dream Part Two!"

"Not hungry but thanks. I'll see how I feel later. Not really up for celebrating," I say.

"We'll just see about that," he says in a baby voice. He gives me a peck on the cheek, promises he'll be home in a few hours and leaves in a rush.

At the party, the smoke machine makes it difficult for me to see more than a couple feet in front of me. The acid I'm on, the smell of the artificially made smoke, it's as if I'm up in the clouds, the ones I used to imagine visiting as a kid when I still believed in the Care Bears. Mom and Sal would be arguing in the front seat of the white Chevette while Max and I rode in back, sticking our heads out the windows like dogs do, trying to convince each other we could see our favorite cartoon characters peeking like shy little children over the fluff in the sky.

When I bump into Kristen, she's as short as a Care Bear but only because she's in a wheelchair. Other than that she's so beautiful, with her short hair and almond-shaped eyes that look like openings into emerald mines, thin, pink lips and bright white smile. God, she's pretty. Too bad she's paralyzed. We were inseparable the last two or three raves. Nick and Ariel would always leave early to fuck girls they'd met at the parties, so it was just Kristen and I by the end of most nights. She always tells me I'm one of the hottest and sweetest guys she's ever met, but I don't believe her. I think she just likes a nice guy around who's willing to push her through the crowd.

She loves to watch everyone dance, always has me stop smack-dab in the middle of the action while I shake my butt behind her and she waves her arms. *Care Bears in the clouds.* She never told me the full story about how she ended up in a wheelchair, something about having weak leg muscles. After being up all night one or two parties ago, a Nor'easter coming on as we rode in Donald's car to an outlaw after-hours in a park somewhere in a Boston suburb, snow pelting us like golf balls, she said that she could walk if she really wanted to, she just had to put in the work, go to physical therapy, but that it'd be too painful and she was too scared to try. She'll get around to it one of these days, she said. But if it's not today then it probably won't be tomorrow—she's in her late 20s. As beautiful as she is, I don't think she'll ever reach her full potential. But who am I to judge? I'm a homeless 16-year-old high school dropout.

Spotting her tonight, I remember the plan we concocted last time we chilled, but had been too scared to try. But now that my other friends have abandoned me and I'm basically homeless again, I'm more motivated to give it a go and convince Kristen to do the same. She only comes to parties after her disability check clears and she can afford to make friends with other ravers by buying them drugs and sometimes taking them for breakfast the morning after a party or for a quick snack before one. Whenever she was broke, she'd call me at Donald and Joann's, crying and lonely. I'd console her, telling her she's gorgeous in spite of everything, we'd see each other soon and party it up.

"You look hot," I say, kissing her moist cheek, staring at the sweat and glitter littering her forehead like fairy feces. "I'm tripping hard."

"I can tell," she says, giggling. "Where are your partners in crime?"

"Gone," I say, too out of it to get angry.

She nods then closes her eyes, moving her head in tandem with the bass of the house music. My shoulders sway. I walk behind her chair, grabbing it by the handles. She's got her hands in the air, and I'm moving her in circles around the dancing crowd, my ass shaking. She's on the Kyle roller coaster. "I wanna try that scam," I whisper in her ear.

"Okay," she says, cackling. "It's early. Let's go to the pharmacy in an hour or so."

Mini Thins are an over-the-counter medication generally used for asthma relief. They're white pills marked with an X. Kristen and I think we can brand them "X-Men" and pass them off as ecstasy. The sales would mean food for me and real drugs for both of us. I wasn't expecting to do this tonight, and the thought of being outdoors in the real world right now freaks me out, but the plan is simple: I'll ask the ravers if they want to buy E, bring them to her, and she'll act as the dealer. After all, what happens if the pills don't work? I mean, what are they going to do, beat up a girl in a wheelchair?

We float toward the exit. Bill the bouncer is showing a hot girl his Taser gun, threatening to zap her. "You better not!" she shrieks.

"Hundred bucks for anyone who lets me Taser them, right here, right now!" he shouts into the crowd. A number of tweaked-out takers speak up.

The 20-degree weather outside greets us like a slap in the face as we exit the hot steamy club. A statue of an alligator stands silently next to the entrance, its mouth wide open, frozen in laughter.

"Hey dude!" yells a preppy kid from the window of a BMW packed with frat boys, stopped at the red light on the corner.

"What's up, dick!" I yell back.

"I'll give you 20 bucks if you hump that alligator you're staring at like you're in love with it. We know you love it."

I'm tripping too hard to be insulted and Kristen didn't even hear what they said. "What?" she asks while I mount the alligator as best I can. I'm humping it and shaking my ass, and the boys in the car are roaring with laughter. The light turns green, they throw a crumpled 20 at me and speed off, one of them belting out, "Freaks!" I guess we are freaks, and before I have a chance to pick up the bill, some homeless man passing by snatches it and runs off. Oh well. We're going to be making big bucks soon anyway.

"Kylie!" I turn and see Wes sticking his head out the door to the party, lollipop in hand, jaw going, forehead sweaty, and wearing *my* visor, which is annoying considering the hundreds he has at home. "Where you going, cutie?"

I smile, trying to mask my irritation. "Be right back!" I say through clenched teeth. "Kristen needs something from the drugstore."

"I'll come with you!"

"No, no, it's private stuff," I say.

He says okay and goes back inside but is obviously jealous, and I don't know why, don't want to think about it, so I shrug it off and start pushing my inebriated friend down the street. I won't depend on him for anything other than a place to stay; if I ask him for money, I just know he'll want to be more than rave buddies. And I don't do that.

The 24-hour pharmacy is like an exclusive club with horrible lighting. There's the regular section where over-the-counter meds are sold, the main space in a club for the common folk, the uglies and the poor. Behind the desk and the glass, in the back room where the brightest lights in the store are shining, the prescription pills sit. The hairy old man in a white jacket, with a nose that looks like a bumpy potato, is the doorman, and he for sure won't let us in, so we glide down the aisle, the shiny linoleum floor freshly waxed by workers on the graveyard shift, so clean it reminds me of my mother's kitchen, and I miss her for a second, but just a second, because then we're in front of the cold medicines: treatments for post-nasal drip, dry cough and mucous-filled lungs. There are other items on the shelves that are comparable to the ingredients in Mini Thins, but we're particularly interested in that brand of asthma-relief medication because they come in pill form and look like real ecstasy.

The old pharmacist won't let us pay for nonprescription drugs at his register; he makes us go up to the front cashier, the general doorman, our money is no good in the VIP section. The Mini Thins cost only eight bucks. I pull a bill from the bundle of twenties Kristen has stashed in the fanny pack hanging off her wheelchair. She's laughing while the fat black chick behind the register gives us dirty looks and pops her gum and every time she does, Kristen laughs harder. I feel paranoid for some reason, so I shush Kristen, collect her change and drive her out of the store so quickly I'm surprised a cop doesn't see and give us a speeding ticket.

Back on the cold stretch of sidewalk between the pharmacy and the Muni, we almost run over the homeless man who ripped me off. He has the nerve to scream out, "Slow the hell down!" and then mumble, "damn kids," as we drive off.

"You owe me 20 bucks, motherfucker!" I say. I hear him hacking up a load of phlegm, and though I'm not watching, can tell he's spitting it at us.

"I'm tired," Kristen says, sitting limply in her chair. Whatever she's on must be wearing off.

"We just need to get back to the party," I tell her.

She nods, then glances at her watch and begins bobbing her head to imaginary music, getting back into the groove. "It's ten after twelve," she says, "We missed New Year's."

"Who cares." I huff. "Should we keep them in the bottle or put 'em in our pockets?" I ask as we near the front doors, the alligator statue snubbing me with a turned-up snout.

"Whatever," she mutters.

I grab a handful of the pills, struggling to shove them down the front pocket of her tight jeans. She giggles, telling me it tickles—proving she has at least some feeling in her legs. I stick the leftovers in the bottle in her fanny pack. Bill will surely search me even though he knows me by name, but he never manhandles her. He just says, "Hey beautiful," smiling widely. He is—or was—good friends with Nick, but

47

whenever Nick wasn't around, he acted as if he didn't know me, and tonight is no different.

Kristen's shiny white teeth have specks of glitter on them; they sparkle under the spotlight that hangs over the doorway of the building. I see the hot girl Bill was flirting with earlier just inside. She's pressing an ice pack against the forehead of some fool who's rolling on pills, to help soothe the wound from the Taser shot. Idiot.

"You okay, chief?" Bill asks me suspiciously. Maybe the acid is making my dark eyes bug out like a French bulldog terrier, or maybe I'm more nervous than I thought.

"I'm fine," I say. He lets me pass, but only after a thorough pat down. I grab the back of Kristen's chair like it's my walker, as if I'm the one disabled, and head inside.

We're about to sell four pills to two goth kids visiting from Worcester. The girl wears black lipstick and has a bloody baby doll in her hair, strangled in a thick black braid like it's the corpse of a suicide victim who slit her own throat and hanged herself at the same time. She tells me she's my age but looks about twelve. I don't want to sell her drugs because she's just a kid, but the Mercedes remote on her keychain and wad of cash in her hand convinces me otherwise. Besides, if she were my little sister, I'd rather have someone giving her fake pills instead of the real shit. She hands the money to her freaky boyfriend. He slips it to me while the girl gets the drugs from Kristen. Someone sees the exchange—a tweaked-out raver sucking on a rubber pacifier with Hello Kitty stickers all over it—so we make another sale, just one pill this time.

"This is so easy!" Kristen says. I spin her chair 360 degrees. Taking the last tab of acid Wes gave me, I push her to a corner where we can both sit.

Less than a half-hour goes by and the tweaker is back. "This is so good, bro!"

"Yeah!" I say. "It's smooth, right?"

"At first I didn't think I felt anything, but then I was sitting there and looking at this sweaty fat chick dancing. I mean, her fucking tits were rolling all around, and I felt this urge to just whip out my cock and rub it all over her fat fucking tits like I don't give a shit." He breaks into hysterical laughter. "And then I was like, holy shit, I'm fucking rolling! I gotta come thank this dude and his chick." He gives me a handshake-hug combo and then scampers away like a happy rabbit searching for vegetables in a misty forest.

We're in the clouds. Kristen is a Care Bear. Guess I'm hallucinating again. A dark mass emerges from the dancing trees that are moving to the beat of thunder and flashes of lightning. "Yo," says the dark mass, grabbing me by the shoulder and shaking it violently. The dark mass becomes a fat Puerto Rican. "Bro. Yo. You the dude wit the pills?"

I sober up a bit. "No," I say, "but I know where to get them. X-Men. They're real smooth."

The fat man thumbs his nose. "Aw, yeah, dope. Well, uh, you into moving large quantities?"

My ears perk up. "Yeah?" I ask. "Like what's a large quantity?" I'm negotiating like a professional. Kristen is the crippled Godfather, and I'm her right-hand man. She sits in her chair a few feet behind me. We exchange looks of excitement, dollar signs in our eyes.

"Bout 40 or 50?" There were only 50 pills total, and we've already sold five.

"How about 45?" He asks how much. I offer him a deal. Before he leaves for the cash machine, I ask, "Are you a cop?"

Giving me an offended look, he says, "Do I look like a fucking cop to you, Peewee?"

I give him the once-over. He's got on saggy black jeans, an extra-extra-large white T-shirt and black sunglasses. I wonder how he sees in here, and if he's the fat one whose sweaty, smelly Nike T-shirt I caught myself wearing after smoking PCP that time. "Okay, okay," I say.

"And you better be for real, dude," the fat man says, pointing a finger in my face so thick it's almost as big as my dick. Adrenaline courses through my veins like I just shot cocaine, not that I know what it feels like, but after watching Bridget do it a couple of times, I have an idea.

"What was that all about?" Kristen asks.

She practically does a couple pop-a-wheelies when I tell her about the deal. Fingering in my pocket the cash we made so far, I say, "I don't know, Kristen. We're about to sell a lot of fake pills to that guy. We already have enough to buy a couple real pills and breakfast after we wake up, right? You can sleep at Wes' I'm sure. He's around here somewhere." In the misty forest. The dark, gray—ouch! "What the fuck?" She pinches my arm again, yanking me down to her level.

"Listen to me, Kyle!" she scream-whispers. "We're doing this. You owe me." I run through in my mind all the nights she's gotten me high, all the mornings she's fed me, and I know she's right. She's family, and we're in this together. And we're talking big money. I told him it would cost 650 bucks.

He comes back. We sell him the fake pills. Easier than I thought. Kristen and I are cheering quietly, giving each other silent high-fives. The goth kids show up again.

"We're not feeling anything," the boyfriend says. "We want our money back."

Smirking, I say, "Look, I don't know what to tell you. It's smooth. Other people who did them are fucked up. Check out that dude over there making out with that fat girl."

"Dude, he's been sucking all kinds of stuff up his nose all night right in front of everybody."

I half-laugh. "I'm not the dealer. I'm just a runner. What do you want me to say?"

He gets in my face. Even though he's probably only thirteen or fourteen, he's bigger than me. I'm high and not ready for fighting. When he demands his money back again, getting louder, Kristen appears, wheeling her beautiful body in between us.

"Get away from my friend," she says. "He doesn't sell drugs!"

"Yeah 'cause you do, you gimpy bitch!" the boyfriend says. As the derogatory words escape from his mouth, a burst of lightning flashes before my eyes and strikes his forehead. He shudders as if he's having a seizure. My eyes come into focus on the wires connected to Bill's Taser. The boyfriend collapses into the goth girl's arms. Bill's hot chick yanks the goth girl by her doll-infected hair while he grabs the stunned boyfriend, throws Kristen a wink, gives me a menacing look and takes out the garbage. Some of our raver acquaintances who are high as shit rush to our sides, asking what the hell happened, who are those people.

"They came out of nowhere!" Kristen cries. They console her, hug both of us. We all start dancing. One of them hands us a couple real pills for free, selling us five more. I'm so excited, I pop three immediately, handing the rest to Kristen.

The rest of the night is a blur as it mutates into morning. Most of the pills I've taken have turned out to be mixed with ketamine, a longtime enemy of mine; whenever I do it I feel like an alien trapped inside a human. I can't move from the bench in the back of the club, can't get my legs to operate properly. No more dancing. The trees fall down, mist clears, night ends, but I still can't get up. God, I shouldn't have done so much! Maybe this is punishment for selling all those fake pills. Wes takes the wheel for a comatose Kristen. Some feeling returns to my limbs. I'm walking with trembling legs, dragging myself out of the Muni like a miner who was trapped in a cave for weeks. The brightness of the morning pains my eyes, blinding me. I'm a bug who's been living under a rock, and I want to go back. Luckily, we're not far from Wes'.

But as we near the street corner, something blocks our way. It could be a boulder, but it's not; it's the fat man with his arms crossed, and he's got his buddies with him: three other beefy dudes.

"Good morning, Peewee. Hope you and your chick had a fun night."

"Huh?" I say, my anxious voice melting into a slur.

"What are you talking about, maaan?" Wes looks at me, and all I see is my fucking visor on his head, that thief. One of the fat man's cohorts is searching through Kristen's belongings. He finds what's left of her half of the cash, along with the bottle of Mini Thins.

"Well look at what we have here!"

"Listen, Kylie, I'm just going to wait at the house," Wes says, running off. Kristen's slumped in her chair in a K-hole, completely oblivious to what's happening.

"Take her to the van," instructs the fat man. One of the others grabs her wheelchair, riding on the back of it downhill toward the parking lot. I use what little energy I have to go after her. The fat man catches me by the back of my hair. "You stay put, Peewee."

Falling back, I hit my head on the pavement. It doesn't hurt too badly because I'm so wasted. But then the fat man's boys start kicking me in the ribs. After they're through, the fat man sits on top of me, and that's the worst. He weighs a ton, I can hardly breathe. Grabbing the front of my T-shirt and pulling me toward him, he says through clenched teeth, "Next time think twice. This ain't good for your life expectancy." Spittle wets my chin. A light rain of saliva comes down with his fist.

Morning fades away and becomes night again. The sounds of house music and someone snorting drugs wake me, but not only that. I feel someone yanking down my pants, slobbering on my balls, teeth scraping my cock. Opening my eyes, I see my visor bobbing up and down. Wes is sucking my dick.

"What the fuck are you doing!"

He looks offended, wiping his mouth with a trembling hand. "It doesn't feel good?"

"I don't want you sucking my fucking dick, dude! What the hell is wrong with you!" I hop to my feet, pulling my pants up. Snatching my visor off his head, I smack him across the face with it so hard he falls to his knees and starts tearing up.

"I'm sorry, Kylie! I don't know what's wrong with me."

"I'm getting the fuck out of here right now. Where's Kristen? What happened to her?" Frowning, he grabs me by the ankles as I go for my bag of clothes under the bed. Kicking him away, I make my way toward the door.

"Please don't go! Please don't go! I'll give you drugs. You can stay here for free as long as you want! I won't touch you again, I promise! I'm just lonely."

"I don't give a shit," I say, opening the door. "If you follow me, I swear to God I'll kill you." My voice sounds deep and tough, but inside I'm kind of scared. He's twice my age, and I can't help but feel as if I've been violated.

The first thing I need to do is go find Kristen. On the elevator ride down, I touch my face, feeling the swelling. And my ribs are killing me. I run through the brightly lit lobby and out into the dark night. It's as if the night never ended, and I guess it never does for losers like me.

Racing past the Muni and down the hill, I reach the empty parking lot seconds after leaving Wes'. No cars are on the streets. It must be well past two or three in the morning. Unless there's a party, it's always a ghost town around here this late at night. There's a dark mass in the corner of the parking lot, thick branches from a bare elm tree shadowing it, blocking the glare of the streetlight. The shape of the dark mass looks familiar, and when I realize what it is, I'm horrified. It's not the fat man or his friends—it's Kristen's wheelchair. My heart beating, I find some change in my pocket, along with my cut of the fake-drug money we made last night.

I walk to the pay phone on the corner. Hoping to God Kristen's home, I dial her number, but it just rings and rings. Maybe the chair isn't hers. It could be anyone's. I'd wait around, but it's late. There's no sense in going anywhere now, so I walk back to Wesley's building and push all the buttons on the intercom except for his, someone eventually buzzing me in. Taking the stairs all the way up to the top floor, I set up a makeshift bed with my clothing just outside the door to the roof. It's freezing but not as cold as it is outside, and after living with Donald and Joann, I'm used to it. It's the dead of winter; no one's going to come up here, anyway. I fall asleep quickly and dream of nothing.

Nudge. It's such a funny word. I imagine fudge-covered fat, my finger poking, prodding and squishing it. But then I realize I'm not making any sense, that someone's just nudging me, trying to gently wake me. The fluorescent light on the wall behind Wes looks like a halo around his head. His face is worried and apologetic like that of a dog, a son of a bitch.

"Kylie, you okay?" My face and ribs are killing me, and it's hard to move, let alone sit up. I wonder how he figured out I was up here. "My super was in the lobby telling one of my neighbors a homeless boy was sleeping in the stairwell," he explains, as if reading my mind. He takes a step backward down the stairs. "I'm really sorry about what happened. I was high as a kite. I don't want you out on the street because of what I did. Please stay with me till you figure things out." He looks me in the eye, promising not to touch me again.

Nothing he says matters to me. I don't forgive him, but I have nowhere else to go. Tiffany, that lying bitch, is no longer an option, so I say okay and take the keys to his apartment.

...

A couple months go by like fast cars: a blur of colorful raves, travelling throughout Connecticut and surrounding states, doing drugs on roads, dance floors and in Wes' apartment.

Falling asleep on Wes' couch, I dream of San Diego: the beach, Nick and Ariel. Bass wakes me up, the night back again. Wes dims the lights while singing along to the house music playing, "Women beat their men. Women beat their men. The men beat on their drums." Sashaying into the bathroom, he says it's his birthday and he's throwing another house party tonight. A strobe light is flashing an epileptic's nightmare in the bedroom while a housekeeper is tidying up the rest of the place with her head down. I didn't hear her come in, and before I know it, she's left without having said a word.

Wes gets out the shower, the bathroom door having been open the whole time he was in it, and chitchats with me as he primps and dresses. I tell him happy birthday, he shakes my hand in such a suggestive and creepy way it almost feels worse than the blowjob. I bet it's not even his birthday, just an excuse to party. The shower I take is much quicker. When I come out the bathroom, a clean Adidas T-shirt is waiting for me on the bed. It's too big but looks cool, so I put it on anyway, along with my smelly dirty JNCOs.

White lines are on the mirrored top of a long coffee table in the living room. All the raver boys and girls are sitting on the couch, heads bent, noses snorting, not one of them asking what drug they're taking.

DJ Oskar, who's supposedly a big deal right now, shows up. Wes knows a lot of people, mainly because he's generous with drugs and gets friends into parties for free—but as I learned when I first moved in, it can come with a special price. He walks me around introducing me to people, or points at me when I'm across the room. I see his gay friends patting him on the back and I try to ignore it, take a couple pills someone has given me, and dance to the hardcore house DJ Oskar spins. But then I trip over some guy sitting cross-legged on the floor and fall over, landing on my side. No one asks if I'm okay, and I don't get up. Turning my head, I see Wes leading a boy who looks about 11 or 12 into the strobe-lit bedroom, a couple of the gay guys following and shutting the door behind them. The guy I've landed on nudges me. He doesn't say anything, just pokes me a couple more times till I look up.

"Paul," I say, recognizing him from school.

"Kyle Mason," he says with a smile. "You look fucked up."

"Aren't you?" I ask, laughing uneasily.

"Just a little drunk. Everybody at school is talking about you, you know."

"Really?"

"Uh yeah, dude. Your brother died just a couple years ago, and now you've bounced and you're mom met with—"

"Wait, my mom?"

"Yeah, she came to the school and talked to everyone. She was showing your photo around, asking if anyone seen you."

The chemically induced fun I was just having has morphed into nausea and a desperate need to vomit. I rush to the thankfully unoccupied bathroom to puke. I don't know if it's the drugs I've taken or the surprising news, but whatever it is, it's making me spew chewed-up cereal, beer and bile. I keep heaving, but nothing else comes out. The hallucinating effects of the drugs kick in. I imagine myself as a skeleton covered with just a thin layer of skin, no blood underneath, the blood is gone, and there are no organs except for the heart, which doesn't work anymore. It's like a sun-dried tomato. But I bet it's still a little moist, has a few drops of juice left, just enough for me to squish it. Nudge. Knock.

The door knocks, not really the door. Paul's knocking, insisting on coming in. He doesn't ask if I'm okay, just closes the door and sits on the edge of the tub, staring at me like I'm a new pet. Sticking my head in the sink, I open my mouth under the running water while examining him: his chubby cheeks, nice puffy lips, thin body, big clear eyes, their color I'm unsure of because it's too dark in here; Wes replaced the regular bulb with a red one.

Paul's always been part of the alternative crowd at school. Everyone thinks he's a weirdo, but he's hot so he gets away with it. Last I knew he was dating Courtney, one of the prettiest cheerleaders at Harding. He looked strange next to her, with his septum ring and baggy pants, dark clothing and dirty hair. I've always liked him, though. Not that we've ever spoken before tonight, but I'm not surprised he knows who I am; everyone knows me as Max's little brother.

"So Mason, what are you doing all the way up here, and at Wesley's no less?" I don't answer right away because I'm busy envisioning my mom at our school, wondering how my old friend Fiona reacted to her speaking to the class.

Fiona. That fat bitch. She's white but acts black, has her hair dyed black and pulled so tightly into a ponytail it's as if she had a premature facelift. We were best friends, but that all ended on Rose Day at school. It'd ended well before that, actually. Whenever I'd say no to doing something with her or for her, she'd retaliate in some way. She was a big girl—and I mean huge—so it was good having her as an ally. Everyone was scared of her, and if anyone had fucked with me, she'd have fucked them up. But our so-called friendship came with a price, and when I told her I didn't want to be her errand boy anymore, I found out just how much. She cut me off completely, sealing the deal on Rose Day, a yearly event at our school when you secretly buy a rose for someone and they find out it's you once they get it with a little note attached. The girls get the majority of the roses, the prettiest chicks competing for who has the most. It's dumb. Fiona sent a rose to Ben, one of the most popular guys in our class who'd always said hi to me out of respect for Max, at least until he got the rose—the rose that Fiona had sent but signed my name. Ben no longer said hi to me. He and his friends would look at me across the parking lot and laugh. They wouldn't beat me up, at least not while Jack and my brother's other friends were seniors. Maybe if I had stayed in school this year they'd have messed with me more—another good reason not to go home.

"I don't know," I say to Paul. "No one really cares, other

than not having Rose Boy around."

"Oh c'mon, dude," he says, shrugging. "Everybody knows that Fiona chick sent the rose. She transferred to another school by the way." It feels good to hear someone say they know the truth. I never took the time to deny the rumors, just let everyone believe what they wanted.

"Then why did all the guys talk shit?"

"Because you're beautiful, and it makes them uncomfortable," he says, looking me in the eye. A warm teddy bear hugs my stomach.

"Yeah right," I say, touching my swollen cheek.

"You remind me of a monkey," he says. "That's why I love Courtney so much. I have a thing for monkeys." I don't know what that means, but the word "beautiful" sticks in my mind.

I've always just assumed I was ugly. Especially my nose. It's too big, which is why I always sit in the backseat if there are other people in the car besides the driver. When I have to sit up front and there are people in back, I ride the whole trip with my chin resting on my left hand, the palm of it covering the side of my nose, so no one can see my profile.

There are monkeys in Paul's hair. Jumping out of his greasy curls, they grab onto the shower curtain, hopping from one flower print to another till reaching the top, swinging off the rod and diving into the darkness behind the curtain. Paul is waving his hand in my face.

"Whoa, I'm tripping," I mumble. He cups my face in his hands.

"It's okay, dude," he says, pressing his lips onto mine

and opening our mouths.

It's my first kiss. I mean, I had another first kiss, but it didn't feel like this. I was thirteen, my girlfriend sixteen. It was Amanda, one of Bridget's friends, another slut who'd done sex videos for money with the creepy crippled guy who lived next door to Bridget; at least those were the rumors. Neither of them ever fessed up, though. But like Bridget at the time, Amanda was a lot of fun—another crazy alcoholic drug whore everyone liked to be around. We made out in my basement a few months after Max died. She tasted like cigarettes. I had my hand up her shirt, my pointer finger tracing circles around her hard nipples, but I pulled back when she went down my pants, and she left in a huff. I lay in bed feeling like a failure, waiting to hear from her. Eventually, she called me that night. I heard a boy laughing in the background.

"Amanda?"

"Kyyyllle," she taunted. "I'm about to suck some cock."

"Why are you doing this to me!" I yelled into the phone.

"I'm not. You did!" she said, hanging up in my face. This moment with Paul feels nothing like that, and I have no reservations. It's my hand that's creeping toward his crotch, and he's the one stopping it. Pulling back, he licks his lips.

"Mm, vomit," he says. Turning red, I cover my mouth with my hands and race back to the sink to rinse more, this time using toothpaste. He laughs out loud. "I'm only joking, dude. Can't taste anything."

Courtney comes to mind. She whips open the bathroom door, throws a disapproving look at him and eyes me with disgust. "What are you two doing in here? I knew it was true,

Rose Boy! I'm telling everyone." But she's not really here. I ask him about her.

"I'm still with her, sort of, but kind of sick of it. Guess I just want to take a break for awhile...maybe chill with you again."

"Yeah, I'm down," I say, smiling. He stands, helping me to my feet. A line of frustrated partiers greets us when we open the bathroom door. Glancing at the clock on the wall, I realize it's already after 6 a.m. The party is dying down. DJ Oskar's gone. A mix tape is playing loudly from Wes' expensive-looking stereo system. Paul's holding my hand, guiding me toward the front door. "Wait, where are we going?"

"To my house," he says. "You shouldn't stay here." He lives in Stratford, just one town over from my mom's.

"What about your parents?"

"It's just my dad and he doesn't give a shit."

"I don't know."

I hear loud banging noises coming from the bedroom, deep voices laughing, see the strobe light flashing underneath the door like someone's in there getting electroshock treatments. Maybe it's supposed to be this way. Maybe Paul came here to save me. The smoky loft, the ravers walking through the living room like lost souls, the demons in the bedroom torturing a child, Paul is a saint, an angel, and we fly away so quickly, drive away in his beat-up Toyota pickup so hastily, I forget my visor and bag of clothes.

The burning ash on the tip of the cigarette I'm holding matches the color of the rising sun reflected in the passenger-side mirror. There's no one in the backseat so no need to hide my profile, but I sit sideways anyway in case Paul looks over. I need to remain the beautiful monkey in his eyes. My own eyes get heavy, I fall asleep, dream of Kristen running, the fat man chasing after her but never catching up. She chucks her now useless wheelchair in his path. He trips over it, landing on his fat face, screaming in pain. There's so much blood pouring down his forehead, it's as if a crown of thorns is pressing into it.

I wake up to Paul screaming. We're swerving all over the highway, horns from other cars honking. At first I think it's ice on the road, but when I see smoke rising off his leg, a small fire on his jeans, I quickly realize my cigarette is the cause of the commotion; I must've dropped it when I nodded off. He pulls over in the emergency lane, runs from the car at lightning speed and jumps in a pile of leftover snow. I open my door and walk over, groggily. The hallucinating part of my trip is almost over, but I still feel dazed. He gives me an unhappy look as he stands, the hole in his jeans about the size of a tennis ball, so close to the crotch I can see through to his hairy thigh and the bulge in his tight white underwear.

"Sorry," I say, unable to stop staring. I walk over to inspect the damage and check for burns. He steps back, doesn't seem to want my hand near his dick. He says he's fine, it only hurts a little, he just wants to get some sleep. As we walk back to the truck he throws his arm over my shoulder like a brother, chuckling a bit.

"These were my favorite jeans, dude!" he says, opening the door. I notice they're just as dirty as mine, bet the oiliness helped ignite the fire. If I ever pulled something like this at home, Sal would've ripped me a new one. I'm Paul's monkey, and his forgiveness makes me never want to go back.

The freezing wind coming off the water in Long Island Sound hits me in the face as we make our way from Paul's truck to his family's tiny beach house. It's so small, basically a shack, reminds me of one of those hotdog stands on the beach in summer. Inside, the house is messy, but not dirty, just cluttered, which is to be expected considering how small it is.

His father's sitting on the couch smoking a pipe. He looks like a drunk: fat, unshaven and cranky. He grumbles something at Paul who introduces him as Frank.

Frank stands, tipping an imaginary hat. "Seasons greetings. I'm going to bed," he says, walking toward a room in the back of the house and shutting the door.

"Looks like he's just getting home from a night of partying too," I say. "Where's your room?"

Paul points to the couch in the almost nonexistent living room, which is barely big enough to fit the loveseat and 13-inch TV in it. "Frank and I take turns in the bedroom, but I usually just let him have it. I like it out here." He collapses on the laundry-covered couch, pats a cushion beside him. "C'mon, Mason. Let's just sleep."

Nervously, I sit down next to him. I've never slept so close to anyone, just those times when Jack and I played that pretend-rape game and I got my first hard-ons, but after we'd finished playing, he would always move a few feet away to sleep on his own. Grabbing me by the waist, Paul pulls me down, draping his right arm over me. He falls asleep and starts snoring almost immediately. With Frank's loud wheezing in the bedroom, it sounds like they're singing me a lullaby, or maybe I'm still high. "Whatever," I whisper to myself, feeling safe and content for the first time since Max died.

...

Frank's just gotten home wasted, and he's punching Paul because he thinks Paul's some guy from the bar. Paul's covering his face with his arms, but he's not fighting back. After a couple minutes Frank tires out, throws up all over the kitchen and collapses on the floor. I fill a plastic grocery bag with ice for Paul, then help Frank to bed and mop up the puke.

Paul and I just split an Oxy and are sitting arm-to-arm, watching the TGIF lineup, drinking beers, and eating pieces of an extra-large pizza that Frank bought us as an apology. He blacked out, he said he didn't know, and we understand. Paul's not mad, he still loves Frank, and I love Paul, and we're all happy.

I hear the electric doorbell ring, but Paul doesn't; the volume on it is really low. Moving the shade aside, I peek out the window and see who's out there but don't want to acknowledge her, don't want to tell Paul his chick is here. Then the cunt knocks on the door, and Paul hears it, and that's that. He lets Courtney in; she hugs him tightly. He doesn't seem too enthusiastic about seeing her, which is comforting.

"What are you doing here?" he asks in slightly slurred speech.

"I just miss you so much, baby," she says, then notices me sitting here. "Kyle! Wow. Everyone at school thinks you've been like kidnapped or something."

"Nope," I mutter, "I'm right here."

They grab a couple beers and come sit on the couch with me. We watch sitcoms, none of us laughing or saying much. Frank comes out of the bedroom and leaves for the bars. Before I know it, Paul and Courtney are fucking in the bedroom.

...

Ever since that cheerleading slut from our shitty high school started coming by, I've been seeing more and more TV and less and less Paul. I walk on the beach a lot, too, wondering if I should tell him how I feel even though I don't really know what's bothering me so much. But the whole thing is kind of bullshit. I mean, why did he snatch me from Wesley's and bring me to his house, introduce me to his father, sleep with me at night for the past few weeks, and make me feel loved when all he really wanted was a monkey, a pet for a little while? Now he's out all the time with Courtney at the football games he claims to be so against, and stopping by the Abercrombie and Fitch store where she works in the mall. Plus, he got a job at Hot Topic, which is in the mall too. I just don't get it.

It's around midnight. Frank is out and Paul's just walked in drunk and passed out on the couch. Rather than telling him how I feel I'm going to show him. I pull down his saggy jeans and start sucking his soft dick, just like Wes did to me. He's getting hard so he must be awake, and he's not making me stop. I've only been doing it for a couple minutes, but he's already coming in my mouth. The come tastes weird but good, so I swallow it. I fall asleep with my head resting on his thigh, my face centimeters from his swollen dick and drained balls.

I'm waking up to doors slamming, and Frank hung over in the bedroom yelling at Paul to stop the banging or he'll bang him.

"What's going on?" I ask, rubbing my eyes. Paul looks in my direction but doesn't make eye contact.

"You need to move out. I'm going to work. Sorry dude." I'd rather have Donald hit me with a brick than hear those words coming from Paul's mouth. Max immediately pops into my head; I remember the blood on the street, the gun. Paul's words are the bullet, and Max is dead all over again.

Apparently, yelling is not allowed in the mall.

"You can't just kick me out!" I scream at Paul.

"Dude, I'm straight. Courtney is my *girlfriend*. This is getting too weird."

Guess kicking displays of vampire teeth and dog chain jewelry, black makeup and Marilyn Manson merchandise, isn't allowed either. Paul's eyes are bugged out, and his face is red. I hear keys jingling on the mall security guard's belt as he rushes into the store.

"If I see you again I'll beat your ass," Paul promises, looking me in the eye.

The guard grabs me by the arm and ushers me out of the store, toward the mall exit. Thank God hardly any shoppers are here yet; there are mostly just employees standing at the entrances to all the stores, gawking at me, including Courtney in front of Abercrombie and Fitch.

"Kyle?" she says, looking shocked as the guards drag me past her.

I turn away in shame, feeling as if I'm on my way to the penitentiary, wondering if this is how they took my dumb murdering motherfucking father to his cell.

"You're lucky we don't the call the cops, kid," the guard says as he shoves me out the door. "Don't come back."

I walk to the bus station, thinking more about my brother and not sure why. Then Mom gets into my head, making me feel worse. My mother. I know more about her at 16 than most kids learn about their parents in a lifetime. But I guess I can't blame her for it. It's not her fault that she was molested by her uncle or that her mom went psycho and died of some brain disease when Mom was eighteen, or that she had grotesquely crooked teeth until she could afford to pay for braces herself because her dad had been too cheap to help, or that she had two kids before she was 20 and regretted it, or that she's estranged from her brother because he's an alcoholic who beat her up when they were kids, not to mention his wife now, or that she was in and out of the hospital because my real father used her as a punching bag until his coke-addicted, retarded self tried robbing a bank and ended up accidentally shooting some kid, and now he's in prison and she's remarried to my dickhead stepfather who strapped her with two more kids, and who she married because he'd been in the Air Force, then got a real job at the silicon factory and seemed like he'd be a good dad, which I guess he is to Mark and Theresa but not to me, especially not since Max died, and Mom's been shitty too. But it's not her fault. It's not her fault she's fucking someone just a couple years older than me and erased any evidence of Max in our house, our lives. There are no pictures, and we can't talk about it. He never existed, just this fresh hell does, it's always been hell, but now it's fresh, and it's just me and her and Sal and Grandpa and the newbies, and it's not home, it's where I come from. But now that Paul's bailed and Kristen's missing and Nick and Ariel deserted me, I have nowhere else to go but back there.

There's a payphone in the Miami Subs restaurant at the end of the parking lot. Finding some loose change in the greasy pocket of my dirty jeans, I pick up the phone and call Kristen's house. It's the third or fourth time I've tried calling her these past couple months. I don't know where she lives; otherwise, I'd have gone over there. The phone rings four times before someone picks up, not saying anything.

"Kristen?"

"This is Kristen's mother, who's this?" she asks. I tell her who I am, she's silent for a few seconds. "Kristen can't come to the phone right now."

"But she's there! She's home? Is she okay?"

The deep-voiced woman sighs dramatically. "Thank you for your concern, Kyle. I'll let her know you called." And before I have a chance to tell her I don't have a home let alone a phone number where I can be reached, she hangs up. It's just my ear and the loud drone of the dial tone.

SPRING

I don't want to go home. I don't want to face her, can't. I don't think of it as home, never have. It's just the place where I grew up, as if I were a maggot born on a decaying animal, and when the maggot got its wings, it flew away and found a pile of shit to throw up on and eat and make babies of its own, then get murdered by the same red plastic swatter that killed its mother, its body parts caked onto the weapon like smashed raisins. There's no such thing as home.

The seasons change so quickly from winter to spring, it's as if the trees were never bare and temperatures never freezing. As Jack and I trail behind a school bus stopping on every corner, I study the trees along the sidewalk, their branches decorated with bits of green and white, buds of leaves and flowers peeking out like a dog's lipstick-colored cock poking through the bump in its fur. Spring is my favorite season. I used to think it was fall, but now all the cool air and crusty leaves remind me of death. I don't need all those gray days making me feel worse.

Jack is driving his own car this time, not the hearse. He's skinnier than when I saw him last, almost six months ago. The soda cans aren't in his ear lobes anymore, and he's put nothing in their place. They look like they're getting back to their

73

normal shape but are still a bit saggy, the holes big enough to fit a finger. I'm glad he agreed to pick me up from the mall right away; otherwise, I'd be roaming Milford aimlessly.

"So how you been, brah?" he asks, exhaling a cloud of smoke, then passing me the blunt.

"Oh, you know. Getting used to the idea of suicide."

He chuckles. "You're a psycho, Kyle."

"Don't forget to go around to the parking lot behind Bridget's. I don't want my mother seeing me."

I had to call Bridget from the payphone to apologize and see if she'd let me back in the dorms, which was obviously out of the question, but she said she was on her way home for the weekend and I could crash at her parent's house for a couple days. She also told me my old bosses at Congress Rotisserie have been trying to get ahold of me. I called to tell them I quit when I moved to Manchester, but I guess they figured out I'd been stealing from them.

"I know I already mentioned this, but I'm packing and leaving in a week, so it doesn't make sense for you to stay with me," Jack says, his eyes glazing over.

"I get it. No worries." He's moving to Portland, Oregon with my ex-girlfriend, Amanda. I remember Bridget telling me at Central that Amanda's become a bigger party girl than she is, which is saying a lot coming from her. He brings his left arm to the steering wheel just as I'm looking over. "Yo, what the hell is that?" I say.

"What?" he asks, following the direction of my eyes. "Don't worry about that." He pulls down the arm of his long-sleeved T-shirt, covering up the yellow black-and-blue hole leaking a little bit of blood and pus. "Just an infection," he says, staring straight ahead, not blinking. "Doing too much."

"Dude, you should go to a hospital. I'll go with you."

"Don't worry about it, little bro. 'Manda and I are going together when we get to Oregon."

"Doesn't it hurt?" I ask, frowning. He breathes in.

"Yeah, I need to go to the doctor's. Just not yet." I spot my mom's little white car parked in the driveway of our house and Sal's van on the street.

"Go fast!" I say, crouching in my seat like a hermit crab. He makes a left into the parking lot behind the condos. "You want to come in and smoke?" I ask. "Bridget's stepmom Diane always has weed."

"I gotta get back. Let's meet up before I go, though."

"Get your arm fixed, please." We bump fists and I get out, knowing I won't be seeing him for awhile, if ever again.

...

"You poor, poor boy," says Diane in a raspy voice, blowing out a huge cloud of cigarette smoke. We've just finished talking about my adventures on the run, and of course, my older brother. She's asked me about his death every time I've been over here since it happened, which was over two years ago. She says she's only 36, just a year older than my mother, but she sure as hell doesn't look it. Maybe she really is the same age as my mom, but if she is, the booze, smokes and coke have really taken a toll. She reclines awkwardly on a corduroy La-Z-Boy, a dingy pink slipper hanging for dear life onto an extra-large big toe. Her legs are stubbly, and she's naked underneath a pale yellow bathrobe. From where Bridget and I are sitting on the faux-leather couch that has holes from cigarette burn on the arm, I can see through a small opening in Diane's robe to one of her saggy tits. She's not overweight and may have been cute once, but she's cut her hair short with bangs, which look strange on her shiny bowling-ball face, her eyes so dark and empty, it's as if you can stick two fingers in them and a thumb in her mouth, roll her down a lane and hit a strike.

"The school's getting Boar's Head meat next week instead of the shit cold cuts we usually have to feed the kids," she boasts. She works part-time in the cafeteria at the elementary school up the street.

I've been over to Bridget's house to get high a few times before, and every time, I've felt a little disgusted with all of us. Maybe it's because Diane does coke by sucking it down her throat with a straw; she tells us she has to do it that way because the doctor said her sinuses are destroyed. "Stevie Nicks loved coke and look at her now! I'm telling you. I'm so much more creative when I do it. I'm painting..." She inhales another line without coughing or taking a sip of wine to wash it down. "And so what if I have to do it this way?" she continues, puffing on a Benson and Hedges cigarette. "I'm not hurting anybody. I still get Caroline to kindergarten every morning and go to work, don't I?"

Bridget and I exchange smirks, quietly giggling while Diane blabs on. Diane's about to fix us our lines when I hear a horn beeping outside and someone pulling into the parking lot. Peeking out the window, I see Bridget's dad's truck and alert the team: "Chuck's home!" Diane hops out of the recliner so quickly you'd think a rat was crawling up her butt. She grabs the plate of coke and runs into the bathroom. Bridget turns on the TV, playing with the antenna until a snowy episode of *Boy Meets World* comes on. Chuck swings open the front door, drops his tool belt on the ground and unties his carpenter boots. He glances in our direction and grunts.

"Diane!" he hollers.

"Daddy! Daddy!" screeches Bridget's younger half-sister, Caroline, as she fumbles down the carpeted front stairs, jumping into her father's arms. She's taken on the looks of her mother and the body of her overgrown father. I don't foresee a beautiful future for her, but she sure is sweet and oblivious to Diane's craziness.

Diane turns up in the hallway, lipstick freshly applied,

smelly robe traded in for a silky pink nightgown.

"Baby!" she yelps.

He drops Caroline and pulls in Diane, shoving his tongue down her throat. She gently massages his crotch, then pats his butt and fixes her hair. Walking into the kitchen to check on the Ragu and ziti dinner she's been preparing, she sings, "Oh, Kyle! The bathroom is all yours!" I start to say I don't have to go, but Bridget elbows me and gives me a look, and I finally catch on.

The plate of coke sits on the toilet seat, two thick lines ready and waiting for Bridget and me. I do mine, then Bridget rushes in. Chuck makes me follow him into the shed behind the condo for some man-to-man talk. God, if he ever knew what Diane did with us, we'd all be dead. He'd beat the crap out of me, divorce Diane, and Bridget's life would be terminated. He really must be naive or not paying attention, especially considering Bridget's love for weed and dope and history of making homemade sex videos for money with their handicapped neighbor.

"Try one of these bad boys," he says, handing me a stuffed clam from a tray sitting on a dusty bench in the shed. It's pretty cold in here tonight, I can see my breath, but I don't feel as cold as I would if I hadn't done the coke; it always raises my body temperature. It's really good coke too, practically uncut, almost yellow in color. I'm really high, jaw clenched, trying as hard as I can to stop it from gyrating.

"Cold?" I ask.

"Yeah, cold. You can't eat a stuffed clam cold? Be a man. It'll put hair on your chest. Here, wash it down with this," he orders, handing me a bottle of blackberry brandy. My appetite is nonexistent from the drugs, but I use my pointer finger to shovel the stuffing into my mouth, the finger I used less than five minutes ago to rub coke on my gums. Chewing quickly, I wash the food down with the thick strong drink. My face scrunches up as he stares intensely. "You like hanging out with my daughter, don't you?"

"Yeah, she's fun."

"Fun. Right," he says, taking a big gulp of the brandy, "I like you, son. But you and I need to have a talk. We can't let what happened last summer happen again."

What happened last summer was I agreed to ride with Bridget to buy dope in Father Panik Village, the most ghetto area of Bridgeport. I don't usually do heroin, but she was scared to go alone, and I was bored. We got the stuff by cracking the window open—my window—no more than an inch. You have to make sure the doors are locked when you go down there because they always try to steal your car and beat you up, but when you follow the rules, they know you're for real. It was a quick exchange, drugs coming in the window, cash going out. We drove off, made it out of the Village around eleven, were somewhere on Mill Hill Avenue when the front right tire went flat. Neither of us knowing how to change a tire, we had to call Chuck and wake him. He had to be up for work at five in the morning. He was not happy. I haven't seen him for more than a minute or two at a time since then, which brings us up to our current conversation. Inhaling another clam, he makes me do the same. I take a second swig of the brandy, hoping it'll alleviate my coke-fueled anxiety.

"You're going to learn how to change a tire tonight. You can't be a man, driving around with a beautiful girl like my daughter, and not know how to change a fucking tire. Now c'mon." He picks up a giant lug wrench from the dirty ground, using it to usher me out of the shed. In the parking lot, we go through the whole process: jack up Bridget's car, take off a tire and replace it with the spare in the trunk. "Righty tighty, lefty loosey," he recites. "That's all you need to know. The rest is cake."

I remember the saying, but he's done most of the work, and I know I'll never do it myself. Still, it's nice that he took the time to teach me something. I see Bridget in the window, jaw going, laughing at her father and me, while Diane dances in the background to "Go Your Own Way" by Fleetwood Mac, the loud music bouncing off the neighboring condos and echoing down the street.

...

It's for the best. That's what I keep telling myself, but I don't believe it. I mean, the best of what? That's the only thing the note said, pinned to the rope around Chuck's neck as he dangled from a tree in St. Michael's Cemetery, a couple rows over from Max's grave. "The best of what?" I ask myself again, out loud this time as I sulk in the den of Bridget's house. It's not the best for Caroline, getting left with a cokehead mother and slut sister. Bridget's my friend, but I know how she is. I haven't seen Diane or Caroline for hours, and Bridget's back at school. When she got the news, Diane—still drunk and high from last night—ran out of the house with Caroline. It's now late afternoon.

Not knowing what else to do, I pack up my clothes and call this black dude Aaron, one of Max's other friends, asking if I can crash at his place for a few days. He lives in Bridgeport, too, but near Seaside Park, which isn't the safest area. But I need to get out of here. I don't think I can face Bridget's family or attend the funeral. I don't want to go through something like Max's death again. I think of Chuck as strong, tough on me, unlike Sal, who's hard because he doesn't want to be my dad. Chuck only wanted to help me. He only wanted to help his family, too, when he hung himself in the cemetery. "Life insurance policy," Bridget said flatly when I called her at the dorm and said I couldn't understand why someone like him would kill himself. She said he'd been joking about doing it for the past couple weeks. A man like him. When a man like him, a real man of the house, father, husband, loses his job, when he can no longer care for his family, maintain his role as the breadwinner, his rightful place in the world, he falls apart. He'd hurt his back at a construction site, but the insurance company had denied his workers' compensation claim. I remember Chuck saying Sal had told him they always do that the first time. My stepfather would know; he'd been injured twice at the silicon factory: once before Mom had married him, another time a couple years ago, shortly after Max had died. Chuck also said he heard Sal and Mom had separated.

The phone rings. Wanting to ignore it, I lean my head on the window in the den, my left ear pressing hard against the rough water-worn wood. The air outside is kind of warm. Breathing it in as it flows through the screen, I watch the wind rocking the branches of the budding trees, the tall newly bloomed bushes swaying in front of my mom's house across the street. I should answer the phone. But I'm busy enjoying the smell of spring, and the memories it brings back. All those days I spent hiding in bushes, the war games I played with Max and Jack, and the forts we built. One morning we found out some crackhead had spent the night in one of our forts. There were vials scattered around it, and it smelled like piss inside. We also found what looked like human shit under a pile of leaves. The phone keeps ringing.

"Hello." I finally answer.

"Yo what up, K!" Aaron yells into the phone. "I'm comin' to pick you up, so get your skinny white ass out to the lot. I'll be driving up in like ten." When I stand up straight, after leaning my head against the window for the past ten minutes, the blood in my brain levels out, making me dizzy and lightheaded.

"Since when do you drive?"

"Man. Just shut the fuck up and be outside." I agree and hang up. My mom will be home from the restaurant soon; she usually gets in around seven on Wednesdays, at least she did when I was living with her. If I'm going to meet up with Aaron, I better do it now. I throw on a worn pair of large-ribbed gray corduroys I bought at the Salvation Army, with the panels of rainbow-print fabric I sowed into the inseam to make them super wide, and an extra-large "God of Fuck" T-shirt Bridget stole from the merch table at a Marilyn Manson concert.

Last time I saw Aaron, his hair was in dreads. His skin is dark, pretty much black; in the sun it looks dark brown. The Halloween after my brother died, Aaron took me out on Mischief Night. We broke car windows, threw eggs at houses. This old dude came outside when we were doing it, threatening to call the cops. Aaron punched him in the face, not that hard, but I heard the old man crying as we ran away. I thought of Grandpa and was scared of Aaron then. Ariel beating Annie at the diner comes to mind now, too. Aaron's a good-enough friend on a superficial level, but I trust him about as much as I do those Puerto Ricans who stole my bike after a day of swimming with them in a lake at Beardsley Park a few years ago. The 13-year-old I thought was cool punched me in the head and shoved me to the ground and took the bike. That's the second bike I've lost. Some other kids had stolen the first one while I was sitting cross-legged next to it in my mom's driveway. Grandpa just kept asking, "Was it a colored boy? Was it a colored boy?" And it was, but that wasn't the point. Regardless, I have to go with Aaron, an 18-year-old high school freshman; he's my absolute last resort. Not that I should talk.

Aaron is honking the car horn in a metallic blue minivan that looks brand new. His friend Derek slides the side door open, revealing six other guys sitting inside. Derek is part of some gang, and I think he intimidates Aaron the way Aaron does me.

"What up, dog?" Derek says.

"Hey," I say. A huge cloud of pot smoke escapes the car. Derek pushes me inside and slides the door shut. Aaron quickly reverses out of the parking lot, almost running over someone walking by. The car radio is blasting, speakers sounding blown. Everyone's getting loud and laughing, paying no attention to the driver behind us honking his horn. Looking back I see it's my grandpa, his hand pressed firmly on the steering wheel. He sticks his head out the window, a cigarette in his mouth. By reading his lips and the familiar look of hate on his face, I can tell he's yelling racist stuff at us. I just hope he didn't see me get in the van because he'd tell my mother and she'd track me down. She used to hate it when Max hung out with Aaron. The tires peel, and we speed away like a rocket blasting off parallel to the ground. Derek turns up the music even louder.

"When'd you get this car, man? You get a raise at the deli?" I ask. Everyone laughs.

"Nah, dude," Aaron says. "Derek knows this guy. We're

doing a job."

"What kind of job?"

"C'mon man, you ask too many questions," Aaron barks, his voice deeper than usual. "Just shut the fuck up. We all gonna drop off the car downtown and then take the bus back."

"I don't have any money," I say, exasperated.

"Chill," Derek says, "I got you covered."

Fuck it. This car is stolen, but fuck it.

"So what happened?" Aaron asks, "Bridget's dad offed himself in the cemetery?"

"That's cold, man," Derek says, chuckling.

"It's not funny," I say.

"Aw shut up, boy," says one of the other guys in the car, "he's just messin'."

"Let's talk about something else," I say, trying to get the image of Chuck hanging from a tree out of my mind.

Aaron pulls over across the street from the Greyhound bus station. The last and only other time I've been down here was in elementary school when Max and I skipped class and snuck to the mall. We'd stolen some of Mom's tip money while she was sleeping, planning to buy new toys. But we took the wrong bus back and had to call our stepfather to pick us up. He beat our asses right on the street. Sitting in this stolen car now, as a teenager, I don't feel any safer.

"Everybody get the fuck out!" Derek says.

"Not you, K," Derek says, "You ridin' in with me." I'm about to protest but Aaron gives me a look. This is my test to be one of them. As scary as they all are, I know that when it comes to getting protection from being beaten up by the assholes who live in our neighborhood, they'll have my back. Yes, initially it's because Derek and Aaron were friends with Max, but sympathy and loyalty only stretches so far. Max used to go do shit with them all the time, things he never told me about, and I'm realizing now it was stuff like this. Derek puts on a black tie and buttons up his white shirt. "We're gonna park this van down here. We just need to get past the rent-a-pig at the gate and then get it parked. It'll look better with a white boy in the car." I agree to do it, although not sure how a pale white kid in grungy clothes, sitting next to a black driver looking like he's about to go on his first interview after being released from juvy, will look less suspicious. Nodding my head, I keep it all to myself, cringing a little when I see him pull a gun out of a Russell Athletic duffel bag and stick it in the waist of his pants the way they do in the movies.

Everyone gets out of the van, hurrying across the street to the bus terminal. Aaron says there are some good vending machines inside, and he's craving cherry Now and Laters. "You gonna be fine, bro!" he says, wiggling my shoulder, then running off with the rest of the crew.

"Shut the fucking door, boy!" Derek says. We drive up to the garage, the fat security guard barely looking up from his Big Mac as he hands us a ticket, telling us to have a good night. Derek drives into the garage in silence, looking extremely serious, a thin layer of sweat glazing his forehead. His black ass is skinnier than mine. With his sunken cheeks and shaved head and skinny arms, he's like a ninja turtle that lost its shell. Plus, he's only fourteen, four years younger than Aaron and about three years younger than me. I don't know what everyone's afraid of. It's probably the gun, the crazy look in his eyes, the rumor that he beat the shit out of his own mother with a garden hose.

Taking a deep breath and exhaling, Derek eases the minivan into a parking space. I smell barbeque chips. He takes two crumpled twenties out of his pocket and hands them to me for helping out. After wiping down all the handles, steering wheel, mirrors and everything, he grabs his bag.

"Get the fuck out, yo," he says. Walking us toward the exit, he explains that his boy runs a really cheap housecleaning service in Westport where all the rich people live, and that he lifts spare car keys from their homes whenever he finds them. In the middle of the night, Derek steals the cars or uses someone else like Aaron to do it, leaving the cars in this lot with the keys still in the ignition. Then he picks up an envelope of money in a locker at the bus station left by whoever's buying the stolen vehicles—he doesn't tell me who. "If you ever rat me out, you'll be seeing your big bro again real soon," he says, lifting his shirt just enough for me to see the handle of the gun. "Don't be offended, son. This ain't personal. Just keep your fucking mouth shut." We reach ground level and walk outside.

"Wait," I say, "Where you guys going? Aaron said I could stay at his place."

Derek hisses through his teeth. "Man, I don't know nothin' about that, and we got other business to take care of. Just get the fuck outta here. You blowin' up our spot, cracker."

I make eye contact with Aaron in the window of the bus terminal and give him the finger.

The miles-long walk back to my mom's happens in fast-forward. It's bad enough I'm back in Bridgeport—clones upon clones of housing projects, dilapidated duplexes, abandoned lots, deserted warehouses with broken windows and home-less inhabitants of the crackhead kind, a half-deserted down-town, rusty wire fences, bent barbed wire and cracked pave-ment, then boxy ranch-style houses, trees, some bare, some budding, kids going inside for dinner, vans driving by prob-ably used to kidnap, rape and kill little boys and girls, Ohio Avenue where Amanda cheated on me, Pennsylvania Avenue where they murdered Max, and Louisiana Avenue where I grew up—but now I have to go home. I'm not ready for this family reunion, Chuck's funeral, the look on my mother's face when she sees me for the first time in six months.

Walking up to the house, I notice Sal's car isn't in the driveway, so he's either working the late shift or moved out. And I hear no loud TV or sounds of Mark and Theresa play-ing, which means Grandpa's not there, and my siblings are with Sal's parents. The front door to our house is open, just the screen door closed. Peering through it, I see my mother standing over the stove, smoking a cigarette with one hand and stirring a pot of sauce with the other. Looking tired and pretty, she's still got on her apron from work. The overhead fan is circling very slowly, blowing the smoke around the room, and she's taking a huge drag and exhaling as if she's just finished a ten-mile run. I tap the metal door lightly with my pointer finger. She jumps at the sound, turning to look with wide eyes.

"You scared the shit out of me!" she says through a laugh, then quickly tearing up. "Kyle. Oh, thank God. Where have you been?" Unlatching the hooked lock, she opens the door. "You know what, it doesn't matter." She gives me a hug and doesn't let go, even after I let my arms drop to my sides. "I thought I lost you, too. Thank you, God," she says in a barely audible whisper. She loosens her bear hug enough for me to pull away, and I'm feeling nervous and uncomfortable. There's too much guilt and anger between us, holes that will never be filled. She has me sit down, insisting I eat something.

"I'm sorry, Mom," I say.

"No, I'm sorry," she says, poking her head out from behind the door to the fridge. Her eyes tear up again. "Do you want a sandwich? I've got pepper turkey. Or some iced tea?"

"Chuck hung himself in St. Michael's this morning," I say.

...

Mom makes a cake for my birthday, then goes to Chuck's wake with her 19-year-old boyfriend Eric, and I stay home. The pain in funeral homes seeps into your bones like cancer or a Connecticut winter, and I've had enough. I'm starting to think my mother only knows how to be miserable. She's always going to wakes or funerals: one for Max, one that she told me about for the coworker of a customer at the restaurant a couple weeks ago, and now one for the neighbor's husband. She doesn't even like Diane, but in the past week, she's made two trays of baked ziti, a vat of chicken noodle soup and two huge pies: one apple, one ricotta.

"She was nice enough to watch Mark and Theresa when Max died, it's only right for me to return the favor," she says to Eric, who's annoyed she's spending more time cooking and practicing for an interview and less time fucking him. He huffs and goes into the bathroom, probably to take another nasty dump. Ever since I've been back, she's been acting like a combination of Stepford Wife and Mrs. Brady rolled into one Super Mom.

One of her customers at the restaurant is this fat 40-something lady named Gay who works in the office of Local 973, the union for grocery store workers. Knowing Super Mom has three kids and is sick of waiting tables, Gay said she might be able to get her an interview for a receptionist position—Gay's expecting to be promoted to an executive administrative assistant job because the one who had it died of Lou Gehrig's disease a couple weeks ago. Max had done his eighth grade science project on the terminal illness; he'd said it turns your muscles and nervous system into mush, you don't have the strength to hold in your shit or breathe, and then you die. Gay told Mom that the woman who'd died from it had been a real cunt who terrorized all the people working under her; they're sorry for the way she bit it but happy she's gone.

We have an old Dell computer that I found next to a dumpster behind People's Bank last year. It came with a keyboard, monitor and mouse, and turns off randomly, but is good for going online a few minutes at a time. Mom's been using it to sharpen her typing skills. She whimpers over the keyboard, insisting she's dumb and not going to be good enough to get the job.

"Mom, please. You're going to nail it, watch. All the coupons you clip. Your bookkeeping for the family."

"I couldn't even give a speech for my class when I was in high school. I'm not good at this." Sniffling, she wipes her runny nose with a tissue.

"But it wasn't so bad, was it?" I ask.

"Why the fuck do I want to stand in front of a class? I had diarrhea for a week worrying about it…I just dropped out." She punches the keys one at a time, copying an article from the *Connecticut Post* as quickly as she can.

"What did your parents say?"

"Pfft. Your grandpa? He was always working overtime, he didn't give a shit. And my mother was already really sick. She didn't believe in college for women anyway." She doesn't look at me as she keeps sulking and typing. "This is why I'm not making you go back to school, Kyle. I just want you to be happy in whatever way is best for you," she says, her eyes tearing up again. Then she starts sobbing. "I really fucked you kids up, didn't I?"

"Ugh. Mom. What happened to Max is not your fault, and I've made my own decisions. I'm seventeen." She keeps on crying, and now I'm getting irritated. Who is this woman? What happened to my mean bitch of a mother? I don't like this.

"You know your sister was caught shoplifting at the mall the other day, right? How can I blame her? I was stealing bras and makeup with my girlfriends when I was her age." Coming from the bathroom he just stunk up, Eric goes to her and starts massaging her shoulders.

"Babe, I didn't go to college, either. You're beautiful. We'll be dumb together." She doesn't say anything. He kisses her on the cheek, then plops down on the couch and grabs the remote.

I hear a car pulling up. Looking out the window, I watch Sal quickly drop off my brother and sister and drive away. He's been staying with his parents since the separation. I bet he doesn't know I'm back or how much time Eric's been spending here, and I kind of feel like being a dick and calling to tell him.

Lately, I've been pranking Paul. Not purposely. I always want to say something; I just can't bring myself to open my mouth when he answers the phone. Instead, I place the mouthpiece of the phone against the speaker of the stereo in my room, playing his favorite Hole songs, not saying a word—he loves the band as much as I do. I want to tell him it's me and that I miss him, but I keep freezing up.

SUMMER

It's the beginning of July, been in the 90s and humid for nearly two weeks. Mom's had her sun chair set up in the driveway since April, and it won't be moved until September. She says the stronger the sun is, the better. All her friends call her Black Bird because she's so dark. Eric gave her the nickname, and it's stuck. She told me once that the sun helps cover the stretch marks from giving birth to all us "fucking kids" and masks the scar on her forehead, the one that looks like the letter V. Her older brother gave it to her when she was four. Her dying mother put her in a white dress for her first communion. My uncle was flipping a crowbar off the curb, and she wanted to play. It struck her and knocked her out. All she remembered was waking up in the hospital, her white dress covered in red. Her mother had died at home and she wasn't there. No one knew exactly what my grandmother had; the doctors could only say it was some type of deteriorating brain disease. Mom got a ton of stitches, but it still left the scar, reminding everyone to this day that she's a permanent victim of life.

Our cat Smokey died yesterday. When Mom was laying out, he dropped a dead bird on her stomach. She freaked out, screaming till he ran away. Hours passed and he didn't come back. I finally spotted him across the street. I only wanted him to come home when I called his name. He followed my voice, forgetting to look both ways before crossing. Some guy ran right over him. Mom was already at work, and the Chevette wouldn't start, so Eric gave her a ride home. They scraped Smokey off the hot tar and laid him onto a takeout pizza box, his silver coat covered in dark red. He shit himself and puked up whatever was in his stomach. By the time we got him to the vet, he was a dead pussy pizza.

My mother makes me walk to my job at Food Center. She says if I'm living at home and not going back to school, I have to work full-time, and she won't be going out of her way to give me a ride. Her rules are retarded. One minute, I can do whatever makes me happy; the next, there are new and old ultimatums. She seems to forget I registered for GED classes last week, so I'll be able to get a diploma more than a year earlier than my high school class.

Half asleep, I trip over my own feet while beginning the five-mile trek to work, which usually takes about an hour and a half to two hours, depending on how tired I am and how hot it is outside. One of the reps at Local 973, the union for grocery store workers where my mom now works as a receptionist, got me this bag boy job. The grocery store is in a shitty part of Bridgeport, across the street from the more polluted part of Beardsley Park and right next to what used to be a Caldor's department store until it went out of business two months ago. After I walk the length of the park, I have to cross the highway overpass. There's overgrown sunburnt grass and dead weeds shooting two to three feet high out of the eroded concrete sidewalk. From the corner of my eye I see a few mice scampering out of my way.

The only good thing about this particular morning is that Bridget is starting as a cashier. She's done with the spring semester at school and has managed to fail every one of her courses, and doesn't plan on returning sophomore year, which is fine with Diane, who's planning to spend most of Chuck's life insurance on a new condo and God-only-knows-how-much coke; not having to pay Bridget's tuition just means more money for her. Caroline's been staying with Chuck's grandmother in the senior living residences where Grandpa lives.

I had a dream last night that Diane killed Chuck, his so-called suicide a cover-up for murder. It reminds me of the ending to Christopher Pike's *Die Softly*, when Alexa ties her boyfriend to a bedpost and tapes his mouth shut, forcing him to breathe through his nose, his nostrils getting more and more clogged with the eight ball of coke she's holding to his face till he has a heart attack and dies. I love Pike's books but don't really get how they're for young adults. All they do is encourage us to do drugs, fuck and kill people—two of the three I've already done.

I run into Cosmo in front of the grocery store, and together we walk across the huge parking lot. He's in his mid-20s, but he's skinnier than I am and looks like an adolescent. A hoop ring with a little red plastic bead pierces through the corner of his mouth, hanging from it like a nasty case of herpes. His hair is short and platinum blond, and he's so pale, it's as if he's see-through; you have to look really hard to get that he's not bald. I don't think he's albino because he has dark blue eyes and dirty blond eyebrows. He was already working at the grocery store when I started, but I'd met him before, in a parking lot outside some illegal rave. He'd been on acid, playing on the ground with half-dead ants, telling a story to a bunch of kids about how he'd been fucked in the bathroom earlier by a white guy who had a big black cock. I spot an angry whitehead on the side of his nose and try not to look at it.

"Were you at the jungle party in New Haven last night?" he asks, blowing smoke through chapped red lips.

"Nope. I haven't been to any kind of rave in a couple months now. How was it?" He chuckles.

"Mama, I'm still there." Smirking, I take a drag from his cigarette, then hand it back to him. "I hate working Sundays," he says.

"It's only four hours. You'll be okay."

"Well, I would've called out to be with my new man if the McDonald's I ate before the party hadn't fucked my life," he says, erupting into laughter.

"Ha, how so?"

"Yeah, how so Lady Cosmo?" Josh asks, surprising us from behind. I always feel a bit nervous when I'm around Josh and not sure why, especially because we've been hanging out for awhile now. I mean, I'm not scared of him like other people just because of what they say he did, nor do I care he was supposedly just released from a mental hospital. He's never hurt me, he came to my brother's funeral, and I think he's funny. Once he broke into his cheating girlfriend's car and jerked off in the front seat, coming all over the steering wheel, which I thought was absolutely hilarious. Even though he's two years older than me, we were in the same grade because the teachers had kept him back. He'd dropped out a couple months before I did. Now we're both bag boys.

"Daddy, you don't want to hear this story, okay?" Cosmo says. Josh snatches the soft pack of Camels from Cosmo's back pocket.

"Then I guess you don't need your cigarettes," Josh taunts. Cosmo's genuinely annoyed, knowing Josh won't give in until he gets what he wants.

"You fucking men are all the same." Josh lights two of Cosmo's cigs, offering one to me. We all lean against the glass storefront, smoking as if we're hustlers on a street corner in Times Square in John Rechy's *City of Night*. Cosmo picks at something dark encrusted on the collar of his stretched-out periwinkle polo. "Alright, asshole. So last night, I met this mothafuckin' fine Puerto Rican, mothafuckin' Puerto Yes-I-Can. He was so fine. He sold pills and invited me to his car to shoot up."

"Whoa, you're shooting dope, bro? That's fucking disgusting," says Josh, a sickened expression on his cherubic face. His teeth are perfect: bright white, square when they should be, pointy in all the right places. I've never met anyone else with teeth like mine. I wonder if he has a dental-obsessed mother too; just because Grandpa never paid for Mom's braces, she's been making us go to the dentist every three months since we grew our first baby teeth. My sister and brother have braces, but I never needed them. When Max and I were younger Mom would brush our teeth for us and floss us until we bled. "That's how you know you're doing it right," she'd say. When she lost interest, I never flossed again, but I still brush crazily and haven't had a cavity yet.

"Do you want to hear this or not," Cosmo says. "Because you can just give back my cigarettes and let me start my day, thank you very much."

"Calm down, Lady Cosmo. I don't give a shit what you stick in your body. You're still my favorite." Josh folds his muscular arms and dips his head back, getting strands of longish brown hair out of his sweaty face. Cosmo rolls his eyes in slow motion.

"A-ny-ways, we shot up in his car, but it wasn't that strong, so I didn't fall out. Then he started fingering me." I look over at Josh, whose dark brown eyes have enlarged. I can see him getting more and more uncomfortable and think it's funny. "So he gets one finger, two, three in so fast. Before a bitch could even cough, he was wrist-deep!" I'm laughing hysterically, and Josh is smoking silently.

"And what the fuck does that have to do with McDonald's?" he asks uneasily.

"Well, let's just say he didn't pull out a fistful of plums, okay? I was mor-ti-fied." Completely losing it, I drop to my knees, rolling with laughter.

"I think I'm gonna be sick, yo," Josh utters in a queasy voice. From my place on the ground, I see Bridget's flip-flop-wearing feet drawing near. She looks down at me, a frown on her puffy face.

"What the fuck are you guys doing?" she asks.

"Talking about what we're having for lunch," I say through giggles. Josh hands Cosmo the pack of cigarettes and rushes inside.

"Thank you very much, Mr. Man," Cosmo snipes.

"I don't think they're going to let you run the register in flip-flops," I warn Bridget.

"Whatever," she says through a cloud of cigarette smoke. Her eyes are bloodshot, and she's scratching the insides of her arms.

The sun is really strong. The parking lot is radiating heat, turning the air into boiling oil you can see, and I wish I knew someone with a pool, but it's time to go to work. Time to bag groceries. I'll bag next to Josh most of the day, pass the hours chatting with him about upcoming parties and chicks he wants to fuck.

The first thing he says to Bridget when she positions herself at the register in his bagging lane is, "Sup, B. I'm Josh. Nice to *eat* you." She sticks her finger down her throat, acting as if she's puking.

"I have a U.T.I.," she says.

"That's fucking nasty."

"I can feel it oozing right now. If you come close enough, you can smell it too."

"Listen, little bro," Josh says, while making me switch lanes with him, "you need to shave that wannabe mustache and wear clothes that fit you. You're a really good-looking dude, but you gotta unearth that shit, if you're gonna keep being my wingman."

Hearing this, I get butterflies and think of Max. An older chubby Native American-looking guy with a dime-sized zit on his neck is in my and Bridget's lane. He wears a wrinkled, expensive-looking pinstriped suit.

"I'd have to agree with your pal there," the well-spoken fat man says. He smiles kindly; I look away shyly. When I glance back, he's still eyeballing me. I look over at Josh, who's cracking up, thinking I'm getting hit on.

Cosmo, looking as if he's about to pass out, is scanning groceries in the same lane where Josh is bagging. I hope he didn't shoot up anything during his bathroom break. It would suck if they fired him; there'd be no more morning entertainment. The impatient black woman in his lane slams down a gallon of whole milk. Josh kicks Cosmo in the leg. He wakes up, automatically asking, "Paper or plastic?" The woman looks at him sideways, hissing. Josh is laughing, and the fat man in my lane is still staring at me.

"How about you?" I ask.

"Whatever is easiest," he says, handing me a business card. "Say, have you or your friends ever acted before?" The card simply reads "Tom York, Film Producer," with a phone number and email address.

"I played an elephant in a play based on *The Jungle Book* when I was in third grade," I say, half joking, "and Bridget's done some homemade videos." No one else knows what I'm talking about, but she still gives me the evil eye.

"I can act too, bro!" Josh insists as Cosmo perks up, telling us he's performed in drag tons of times.

"Can you finish ringing me up?" the black woman asks. "Shit, like I have all fucking day to listen to your Cracker Jack-ass carrying on." Cosmo stops scanning and just stands there, staring her down, ready to serve his signature "I will cut you"

101

line, when Herb, the nerdy pedophile-looking store manager notices and starts walking over.

"Cosmo!" I whisper loudly, snapping my fingers, "Let it go! Herb is watching." By the time Herb's within earshot, Cosmo's finished scanning and Josh is just about done bagging.

"Here's your change, bitch," Cosmo says.

"Excuse me!"

"I said, 'Here's your change, miss.'" The woman rips the grocery bags from Josh's hands.

"You lucky I'm late, faggot," she says to Cosmo, who responds with a smile. Herb gives everyone an "I've got my eye on you" look, then gets back to making his rounds. Tom claps quietly while Bridget runs his card. He looks me up and down again.

"Your friends are marvelous, so lively. I'm producing and directing an independent film. I'd love for all of you to come for a screen test at my home studio upstate."

"None of us drive," I say, handing him his groceries. All he's bought is peanut butter, a box of Ritz and a bottle of water.

"I'll send a car, of course."

"Why are you all the way down here in ghetto-ass Bridgeport?"

"Trying to retain my lead actor," he says sadly, "but it didn't go so well."

"How much does this pay. It's not porn, is it?" I ask.

"It does pay, and it's not porn," he says, chuckling. "How old are you?"

"Seventeen. I'm Kyle."

"We might be jumping the gun here, but we would need to get your parents' permission if you're cast." I wonder what Mom would say to me starring in a movie. What if this made me famous? *Kyle Mason: discovered in a Food Center at seventeen.* Tom leaves the store.

"Well I don't know 'bout you sluts, but I'll be putting a pause on partying till after the audition," Cosmo vows.

Josh is busy doing pushups.

Bridget's humming while scanning groceries.

Staring at the fluorescent light bulbs overhead, I'm thinking they appear less harsh than usual.

...

Tom lives in Sherman, a small town upstate I never heard of until I met him. He has a little cabin he says you get to by driving down a dirt road off the town's main street. As we near the road he's pointing at, I see tall grass reaching as high as the windows on the side of the post office, wondering why no one's cut it.

I'm going to do well at this audition. I'm going to get this part. Mom's already treating me differently since I told her about the film. She didn't even say anything about me skipping GED class to go to this. We're the same in that way: always wanting to believe things are getting better.

Bridget and Cosmo are in the backseat of the car exchanging blowjob stories, while Josh and I are squeezed tightly in the front with Tom. Tom said his chauffeur had a family emergency, which is why he had to drive the chauffeur's gold Chevy Impala all the way back to Bridgeport to pick us up; Tom lent the man his Mercedes because the Impala breaks down, and the man's family is all the way in Massachusetts. As much as I admire Tom helping his employee, I'm disappointed we can't ride in the nice car.

Big, lush trees border Tom's house. The sun soaks their green leaves in yellow light, filling me with a sense of warmth and excitement. The first thing I see when we walk inside is a giant VHS camera in the corner of the living room, the record light blinking red like a one-eyed demon watchdog.

"Are you recording us now?" Josh asks suspiciously.

Tom's slightly out of breath from the walk up the stairs to the front door, and is the last to enter. He closes it slowly and wipes his shiny, wide forehead. "Yes, well, I think it's fun later on to...the camera captures the entire audition, before and after you actually read your lines." He shuts the blinds, covering the large bay window in the den. "I want to learn all I can about my actors, and that doesn't stop at their acting abilities."

"Got any food?" Bridget asks. She's been smoking a lot of pot these days and eating everything in sight, which probably means she's due for another abortion. Not sure who the dad could be, and I'm betting she doesn't either. Other than that, she hasn't been acting any differently since Chuck died. It's as if it never happened.

"I'll make everyone a sandwich if you'll take a seat on the couch. Copies of the script and character bylines are on the coffee table."

Excited to finally learn the plot of the film, I snatch up the papers and speed-read. The movie is going to be called *Colors of the Rainbow*. Each of our names is penciled next to one of the characters' descriptions. I'm trying out for Jacob, "a smart, charming and outgoing guy, who's just getting started with his sexual revolution and loves it to the extreme." Tom's assigned Josh to Phillip, "the jock type who is so far in the closet that if you opened the door, you wouldn't see him. He starts hanging with the group because of Jacob, who he finds himself extremely attracted to in a big brother/little brother way."

I watch Josh's face change as he reads about Phillip.

105

"What is this? Some gay porn movie? I'm not doing this shit!" he says. Tom walks in with a bowl of Doritos and a two-liter bottle of Pepsi, and slams them on the coffee table.

"That 'shit,' Mr. Quardt, is not, in any manner, the screenplay for a pornographic film. It's a drama that deals with homosexuality, love, AIDS, and is based on personal experiences that are very near and dear to my heart. You are not required to stay if you find any of that offensive or if it makes you uncomfortable."

"Nah, yo," Josh says, standing and pulling up his sagging jeans, "my bad. Let's do this."

Bridget will be trying out for the fag-hag part, and Cosmo's going to audition for the real queeny character. The part of the script that Tom wants Josh and I to act out has a big disclaimer along the top of the page that reads: "This is *the* passionate love scene and needs to be REAL. WARNING: There is nudity in this scene and needs to be handled with the utmost professionalism." Josh's forehead glistens as Tom points the camera at the two of us sitting on the couch. Bridget goes to the bathroom to do whatever shit she's got on her, and Cosmo's already in Tom's bedroom on the computer, most likely in an AOL chat room, trying to plan a hookup.

"Yo, you ready?" Josh asks loudly, his voice sounding much deeper than normal. I nod without making eye contact. Before Tom has a chance to say "action" or whatever, Josh is racing through his lines. "I've wanted to do this for a long time," Josh as Phillip says, awkwardly moving his finger down my chest. His thick finger reaches the waist of my jeans, then pulls away like a turtle that's been spooked.

"Kyle," Tom snaps.

"Oh, sorry," I say, realizing I've missed my cue. "Why didn't you tell me before, Phillip?"

"We're such close friends that I thought it would ruin everything. I'm still not sure it won't."

The script says that Phillip now takes off his pants and underwear, then stands to face Jacob, who's sitting on the couch, Phillip's back—and bare ass—to the camera. Without hesitation, Josh yanks down his baggy jeans and boxers, his big dick suddenly in my face. "Oh believe me, dude. It won't ruin a thing," he says, before busting up laughing.

"Focus! Focus!" Tom orders.

Josh smells a bit ripe with his pants down, but for some reason, I like it. Embarrassed, I look away, catching Tom with his eyes glued to Josh's ass. The door to the bedroom swings open, Cosmo appears, his jaw dropped to the floor.

"Oh. My. Lord and Taylor!" Cosmo yelps.

Josh gives him a nasty look and covers his junk. "Get the fuck out of here, faggot," he says.

"Mothafucka, I know you did not just call me a fa-"

"Maybe we should just clear the room of anyone who's not acting at the moment," Tom suggests, cutting off Cosmo.

"Good idea," Josh says loudly, keeping an eye on Cosmo till he leaves.

Cosmo walks outside and slams the front door shut. "Don't make me call my goddamn cousin, mothafucka!" he screeches. "I will cut you!"

...

This is my second weekend going to Tunnel in New York City since moving back home. Last time Cosmo took me, he was in full drag. We had to stop at a pay-by-the-hour hotel on the West Side Highway, where he'd made plans to meet one of his johns. He had me wait in the lobby while he did his business with a married Haitian dude from Jersey. The dude wanted to fuck Cosmo, but he freaked out once he realized he wasn't a real girl—the first time they'd met, Cosmo had just blown him. When Cosmo got naked, the dude screamed, "You're a fucking guy!" charging out of the room without paying. Cosmo did look pretty believable, I guess, but that hotel was packed full of tranny hookers, so his trick must've been a real dumbass.

Tunnel is a mixed crowd; there are separate entrances for straights and gays. Most people want to go through the gay door because that part of the club is where the better music and drugs are, and if you get in through the gay entrance, you're free to visit the straight part of the club too, but not vice versa. Cosmo says they turn away a lot of guys that look too straight or like they might cause trouble for the real gays and gay-friendly. He always gets into Tunnel right away because he's been going since he was thirteen, so he's already in the club, but they won't let him bring in anyone else underage. Josh came this time, so he and I are both stuck outside, asking people in line who look sort of like us if they have an extra photo ID we can borrow to get in; the club's 21 and over.

Borrowing someone's ID worked for me last time. I had such an awesome time, way better than any rave I'd been to, even the one at that abandoned shopping mall right outside Boston that I'd partied at with Nick and Ariel.

Miss Kitty, a white drag queen with big platinum blond hair, sees us and runs over to pinch both of our desperate asses. "You pretty baby mens! Come on mama, I mean come *with* mama," she says loudly. Everyone in line is staring and cackling. She lets us in without checking our IDs, and once we're inside, introduces us to Joey Flair, the 40-something dude who runs Bedtime, the Saturday night party in the gay section of the club.

"Hey hot boys, how 'bout a promoting gig? Pass these discount flyers out to your friends. Scribble your initials on them, and I'll pay you two bucks for each boy who uses 'em," he says.

"This means we can get in without ID or paying," I say to Josh, but he's too wasted on E to know what's going on around him.

Josh spends most of the night making out with some chick I'm not sure is a real girl. I sit next to them enjoying my high, massaging his thigh and shoulders, while Cosmo vogues for hours in the furry pink room next to us.

Leaving the club, I smell a street vendors' gutter chicken, an ass-scented glaze that a passing garbage truck just left on 11th Avenue, and cocaine up my nose. All the older guys at the club were really generous with their stuff; I'm also on ecstasy, acid and one or two other drugs I can't remember the names of as we make our way toward Grand Central.

Waking up at the New Haven station, I realize we all passed out on the train and missed the stop in Bridgeport. We're about 20 miles from home, with no money to get back. Josh is half awake and in a real shit mood because he's coming down, so he starts punching the ads hanging on the walls of the train, going on and on about stuff that doesn't make sense. "We never have any fucking money! Where's the money! I'm gonna blow up that fucking grocery store, yo."

Cosmo's checking himself out in a compact mirror, completely unfazed by the scene Josh is making. A fat bearded conductor emerges from his little room, telling us this is the last stop and we have to get off, warning Josh to stop punching things or he'll call the cops.

I can't ask my mother to pick us up; she thinks I had dinner at Josh's house and slept over. Having no other choice, I call Diane from a payphone. She picks up on the first ring, laughing out loud when I tell her we missed our stop. It's only 8 a.m., but she says she hasn't gone to sleep yet either, and would be more than happy to give us a ride home. She'll probably be driving drunk, but with the alternative being my mother's wrath, I gladly accept the offer. As much as I'd like to believe my relationship with Mom has changed, things are pretty much the same.

...

Derek has a new tattoo that says "Money Over Bitches" wrapping around his neck. He's more built than he was two months ago. I really didn't want to see him again, but Josh made me set up the deal because he wants new clothes and bag boy pay hasn't been cutting it.

I overheard Josh asking Cosmo if he knew of anyone who'd be interested in buying pills of ecstasy. Josh knows someone in New Haven looking to sell a few hundred of them for really cheap. The dealer is just some rich raver kid who goes to Yale. He's moving home to L.A. and wants to get rid of his supply before he leaves. I called Aaron; Aaron called Derek. The plan tonight is, Derek will pick up Josh and me, we'll drive to New Haven, get the drugs from the rich kid's dorm, bring them down to the car, get the money, Derek will drive off, Josh and I will bring the money to the rich kid, get a cut of the cash and then take the train home to Bridgeport. Easy deal.

I don't really care about the money, but Josh says the dealer is going to hook us up with a few pills of our own, and I'd really like to roll with Josh. Plus, helping him out will only make us better friends.

"I'm going to the movies, Ma," I lie. She's reading *In Cold Blood*, half listening. Ever since she got the office job and started on Zoloft, she's been staying in at night and reading all my books.

"Okay, Kyle. Be careful. If you're going to be sleeping

out, give me a call please."

"Night," I say.

Josh is sitting on the porch smoking a joint. "Dude! Not so close to my house. My mom's going to smell that shit."

"Chill out bro. It relaxes me."

The sun's going down, but it's still really humid out. As soon as I'm outdoors I start sweating. Josh is wearing a dingy white wife-beater, baggy jeans and a chain wallet that's most likely empty. The shoelaces to his beat-up Nike's are untied. I follow him from behind, smelling his body odor. We walk up the street, finding Derek alone in a red Toyota Camry parked in the lot behind People's Bank.

"What up boys," he says, giving us a gold-toothed smile. "How ya been, K?" We get in the car. Josh sits in back.

"This is my boy I told you about. Josh, Derek."

Derek eyes Josh in the rearview mirror, nods his head. "Sup," he says.

The drive to New Haven goes by quicker than I thought it would, Derek passing a blunt around and chatting us up the whole time, discussing music, how he wants to fuck Lil' Kim in the ass, Josh chiming in, the two hitting it off right away. I've never seen Derek acting this friendly toward some-one he didn't know; he's hardly nice to the friends he's had for years. Maybe he's nervous because he's on his own and hasn't worked with Josh's dealer. But then again, that'd be weird, considering Derek knows the dude is just some white Yalie. We park in an empty lot about a block from the dealer's dorm.

"We'll wait here," I tell Derek.

"Oh no you won't boy," he says. "I need someone I can trust keeping your boy honest."

I don't argue, just hop out and follow Josh down the street. "He's not so bad, right?" I say.

"I don't know."

"What do you mean? He's being cooler than I've ever seen before."

"I just get a bad vibe."

"I've known him since we were kids. It's all good."

The security guard at the dorm calls the dealer, whose name is Parker. Parker clears us, and we head into the elevator. This and my time at Central last year is the closest I'll ever get to going to college.

"How do you know Parker?" I ask.

"Met him at a rave."

Everyone seems to meet everyone at raves these days. We walk down the hall, find the room, knock on the door. It swings open almost immediately, a song by Dave Matthews Band playing so loudly inside, it's almost unbearable.

"Joshy boy! My man! Who's your friend?" Parker wears a blue Ralph Lauren oxford shirt and a pair of white boxers speckled with little red lobsters. Standing in the doorway and obviously not feeling obligated to invite us in, he hands Josh a Ziploc bag full of pills that have tiny pink elephant stamps on them. "That's 500. Want to count 'em?"

"Hey, I'm Kyle," I say.

Josh holds the bag up to his face. "Nah, it's all good. I trust you. Be right back with the money."

Getting serious, Parker grabs ahold of Josh's arms and

looks him straight in the eye. "I trust you too, dude. Don't fuck me."

Josh gives Parker a perfect smile. "See you in a few minutes."

"Before I forget, these are for you." He takes ten loose pills out of the front pocket of his shirt and hands them to Josh.

"Thanks bro. Be right back."

We hear bass coming from the speakers in the Camry more than a block away from where Derek is parked. Seeing us near, he turns down the volume, a cocky grin on his face. When he opens the door to get out, he leans on the steering wheel, accidentally honking the horn.

"So how'd it go, yo? They real, K?" he asks, strolling toward us.

Josh lights a cigarette and tosses the bag to Derek. "See for yourself," he says.

Derek rolls the stuffed bag around in his hands, then opens it up and inhales. "Looks and smells good to me."

"So it's five-thousand," Josh says, blowing out a huge puff of smoke. "Hurry up, 'cause the dude is all paranoid, and I want to get back."

I open the passenger-side door and take a seat in the car. As I do I see two black guys coming up from behind Josh and Derek. One gets Derek in a headlock; the other puts a gun to Josh's head.

"Give us the shit or you're dead." Neither of the dudes is acknowledging me. I don't say anything.

Josh doesn't seem scared, just surprised. "What shit? I

have like two dollars in my pocket, man. Take it."

The guy holding up Josh hits him in the chin hard with the gun. Josh holds his hand to his face, blood leaking from between his fingers like an eroded dam about to burst. The other dude doesn't have a gun, but he's keeping Derek in a headlock.

"Here homey." Derek chucks the bag of pills at the guy behind him. "Just stop hurting my boys."

As soon as they get what they want, they're gone. I hear tires peeling, a car speeding away and then nothing. Stepping out of the car, I walk toward Josh, who's still bleeding badly. "Fuck, we need to get you to a hospital," I say.

"Yo, I'm out," Derek tells us, "You's coming or what?"

"Can't you see he needs stitches?"

"I need to go tell Parker what happened first," Josh says.

"Fuck that shit yo. You dumb white boys do what you want, I'm bouncin'." Derek gets in the car and drives off, leaving us alone in the parking lot.

Why didn't they point the gun at me? Maybe it's because I didn't seem like a threat. Part of me wishes I got shot. I want to know what it feels like, what Max felt, and if it killed me, I wouldn't have minded much. "You need to go to the hospital now," I say to Josh.

Wincing, and through clenched teeth, he says, "Nah, I gotta tell Parker what happened. We have to show him."

"But you're bleeding all over!"

"Shut the fuck up and start walking."

This isn't going to be good. When we get to the dorm, the doorman takes one look at Josh and tells him he can't come in.

"I'll just run up," I say.

"Bring him down here, so I can face him. This is my shit," Josh orders, walking outside and crouching down on the sidewalk, leaving behind a trail of dark red spots.

The blood on my balled-up purple T-shirt that Josh has pressed against his face is brown and hardened. The color combination reminds me of bruises and shit. His chin is already black and blue. I almost crapped my pants when Parker and his boys chased us down the street with bats, which is weird because when that black dude had the gun, I didn't even blink. It must be because I'm not afraid to die. But getting cut or scarred or feeling pain really worries me. If I feel nothing, if I get a bullet in the head, I'll just disappear. There'll be no pain. I've got no clue what comes next, but I do know I'm ready.

I sit shirtless next to Josh, who's nodding out. We've been in the emergency room at Bridgeport Hospital for hours. The sun is coming through the floor-to-ceiling windows and steaming us like Chinese pork dumplings. A woman being rushed in on a stretcher is vomiting uncontrollably as an EMT holds a small plastic bag up to her mouth. The woman's sobbing and throwing up, snot and bile coming out of her nostrils every time she heaves. They take her right in back, leaving Josh and I to keep waiting as if we're invisible. He slumps over with exhaustion, unconsciously placing his head on my bony shoulder, exhaling with a slight snore. I scan the room, looking to see if anyone's paying attention, not daring to move my head for fear of waking up my new best friend.

Breathing in, smelling his dirty hair and sweaty body, I'm getting a hard-on. He loosens his grip on the T-shirt, letting his head drop to my chest, his hand falling in my lap, inches from my dick. I look down, study the contours of his face from this bird's eye view: his long eyelashes, strong nose, full lips and cheeks, a shadow of facial hair making his pretty face more masculine. This is my brother. Here in this hospital, suffering this pain together. A warm, wet feeling.

The blood-clotted gash on Josh's chin has cracked open, and he's bleeding all over my jeans. Reminds me of the summer before last, just before Bridget started college, when she walked around for an entire day wearing cutoff jean shorts stained with period blood because she'd been too lazy to get a tampon. She thought it was hilarious buying chips and blunts at the corner store while the waste from her uterus was trickling down her inner thigh like melting cherry sherbet.

"Josh."

"Mhm!" he whines in tune with a baby across from us who's screaming like an opera singer into its mother's tit.

"Josh! You're bleeding."

In a flash he sits upright, a light spatter of blood speckling my bare chest. "Yo, what the fuck? Why you let me fall asleep?!"

"I didn't, dude. It's almost seven in the morning. I was passing out too." *Josh Quardt. Josh Quardt.* "That's you. I'll go with you."

"Nah, just wait out here."

I watch him walk away with my T-shirt on his chin as he goes through the double doors labeled "No Unauthorized Entry."

...

"The barbershop on East Main Street closed down," I say. "I used to get haircuts there as a kid."

"I heard it got raided," Josh says, feeling in his pocket for a lighter.

Snatching the joint from his mouth, I say, "Not surprised. Those cokeheads sure didn't know how to cut hair."

It's 101 degrees; heat's rising off the pavement and making the air look oily. Josh finds the lighter, puts the skateboard he had tucked under his arm on the ground, takes back the joint and rides off. "See ya!" he yells back as he turns the corner on Ohio Ave, cackling. I know he's just waiting on the other side, and I'm already drenched in sweat just walking at a snail's pace, so I take my time going after him. When I finally turn down the street, I don't see him, thinking he deserted me. "Psst!" he whispers. Scanning the houses to my right, I spot him sitting on his skateboard behind a bush. "Get the fuck over here, Kyle!" he says, gesturing crazily. "Quick dude!" I run over and hide with him, not asking why.

This woman tried kidnapping Max and me when we were kids. Mom was pregnant with Theresa. She and Sal had gotten married a couple weeks earlier, and we'd just moved from Grandpa's into our house on Louisiana Ave. The driveway hadn't been paved yet. It was just dirt and rocks, which Max and I used as weapons during battles between his G.I. Joes and mine. A woman standing next to a parked car across the street interrupted our game. She was wearing a brown

119

pantsuit and had short blond hair. "Hey boys," she said, "Is that your scarecrow?" It was a couple days after Halloween, and our neighbors, who have since moved away, had put a scarecrow in their front yard. Max froze like one of those soldiers at Buckingham Palace.

"That's not ours. That's next door," I replied, giggling.

"Oh, well, it's very nice. Say, I have some candy here," she said, opening the backdoor of the car. "Want to go for a ride?" As much as using candy to lure kids into a car sounds like an urban legend, it actually happened to us.

"Run!" Max screamed at the top of his lungs. Grabbing me by the wrist, he yanked me to my feet, dragging me to the backyard as fast as he could. Once we were there, he banged on the locked patio door till our mother, days from her delivery date, let us in. I was terrified. When we came back out with Mom—who hadn't taken us seriously—the lady and the car were gone, and we never saw her again.

I didn't think I'd see those two black guys who robbed us at gunpoint again either. But there they are smoking a blunt, sitting on the stoop of a rundown duplex across the street. It's bad enough running into them, but that's not the worst part: Derek's just pulled up in a black Jeep he most likely stole, and is honking the horn even though his accomplices are just a few feet away. "Let's go, bitches!" he shouts.

I look over at Josh: beads of sweat are dripping off his brow and onto his long eyelashes. He's staring through the holes in the patchy green bushes, eyes locked on Derek. Not only has Derek hurt Josh and played both of us, but he also has the balls to ride around with those guys just two blocks from my house. When I was about six or seven, this pit bull chased me down the street and bit off a chunk of my butt cheek. The dog was white and had black eyes, an empty soul with one goal: hunt and kill. If the owner hadn't caught up with it, it probably would've mauled me to death. Josh has the same look in his eyes. The gossip about him being crazy, the stories people tell about him having spent time in a mental hospital and being extremely violent, they all seem truer now.

"That motherfucker!" he says, standing up.

I grab onto his rock hard leg, trying to pull him back. "Josh, they're going to see us."

He fingers his chin. The scab has almost fallen off, but a thick scar—most likely permanent—is taking its place. "Stay the fuck down yourself," he says, shoving me away. "I'll be right back."

I want to stop him, but I know it'd be pointless because he's much stronger than me. The two dudes have climbed into the backseat of Derek's car. Derek has his head turned to them, the "Money Over Bitches" tattoo splayed across his neck like a flag for a sports team.

Rolling up to the driver's side door, Josh sticks his head in the open car window. "Yo!" he hollers into Derek's ear.

Rather than acting shocked at being caught, Derek just smiles. "What up, son?" he says.

Josh hops off his skateboard, kicks it up into his hands and slams Derek's face with it—wheels first. Derek's head snaps back. Chucking the skateboard aside, Josh grabs Derek's skinny neck with his left hand and pounds him to no

121

end with his right fist, all the while grunting and groaning the way Max and his friends would whenever they lifted weights in our basement. By now the two black dudes, who must be unarmed, have jumped out and are trying to pull Josh off Derek. But like a pit bull whose jaw's locked onto an ass, he won't budge. He's going to kill Derek. Oh my God, he's really going to kill him!

"I called the cops!" a woman shouts from the window of the house next door. I jump out of the bushes and bolt across the street. The two black dudes have given up trying to stop him and are just standing there in shock, watching him beat Derek half to death, horrified looks on their sweaty faces.

...

My father and big brother are gone. I think about Max just about every day. But not my father. I don't care that he's not in my life because I know I wouldn't benefit from having him in it. Not because he's a murderer, but because he's a fucking idiot. I'm embarrassed to tell people he's some dumb druggie who beat my mother and tried robbing a bank, and not only failed, but also killed someone in the process, and not on purpose. Guess I still have my mother, who I hate a little less now that she's working at an office and acting more motherly. But I won't be able to deal with losing Josh. He's the closest I've felt to another guy since Max died, more so than Nick or Paul, and he's sitting in jail right now because of me. If I hadn't introduced him to Derek, none of this would've happened. It's not like we can just come right out and tell the police Derek had his boys mug us for our drugs.

Derek's in the hospital. Aaron says they've got this big metal contraption holding his face together, but I'm sure he's exaggerating. Josh's right hand is broken. After the police took him away, I found his skateboard down the street. He'll be happy I got ahold of it before they did.

Herb, the general manager at Food Center, is emaciated and basically bald except for a few greasy brown curls poking out the sides and back of his bulbous head. His eyeglasses give him a permanently surprised expression, and whenever he's stressed out or mad, he looks less like our boss and more like a serial killer.

"I'm going, Herb. I've got to figure stuff out for Josh," I say, handing him the cash box from my register.

"I've had it with you and that goddamn kid. Your shift isn't over for another forty-five minutes, Kyle!"

"You finish it then! Instead of standing around all day staring at us like a perv."

He slams the cash box on the desk and grabs me by my skinny arm. "Okay, that's it. Let's go."

I try to wriggle free from the psycho, but he has a strong grip. "Get the fuck off me, Herb! I'll call the cops!"

He drags me down the soup aisle where an audience of perfectly aligned Campbell's and Progresso cans enjoys the show, and past the registers.

Cosmo and a long line of customers at his station—the only one open—are staring at the spectacle in silence. "Mama, what's going on?" he asks.

Herb gets me to the front of the store. As the automatic doors slide open, thick, scorching heat from outside suffocates me. "You. Are. Out of here!" he announces like an umpire, throwing me into the satanic summer day, a satisfied look on his goggle-eyed face.

Guess I'm out of a job. Oh well. I don't think much about my future. My mother never really mentions it, other than bugging me to save money. Sure, she wants what's best for me, which to her is finishing school, getting a decent job, becoming self-sufficient and starting a family. I think she thinks I'm gay. She had Eric give me a ride home from the grocery store the other day, knowing how upset I've been over Josh getting locked up.

"Your mother's just concerned, dude."

"I'll bet," I said, making handprints in the blanket of dust on the car's dashboard.

"She just wants you to be happy."

"Since when."

"And that fag, Cosmo. He's a bad influence. You know what they say, birds of a feather..."

A memory popped into my head of when Mom had taken me to get sneakers at Caldor's: she'd been making fun of the cashier because he'd talked with a lisp.

"You don't even know him. And Josh is my best friend. Anyway, you're like two years older than me, so stop acting like a dad and just keep on doing what you do best: fucking my mother and minding your own business."

He didn't say anything else. He just turned the key in the ignition and drove us back to the house.

That was just a couple days ago, so I can't go home right now and tell Mom I've been fired; she'll totally flip. I just need to focus on figuring out how to get Josh out of jail. Considering Tom, I walk to the payphone at the end of the parking lot to call his cellular phone—he's the only person I know who actually has one.

He says "mmhm" and "uh huh" as I talk furiously.

"Is there anything you can do?" I ask, sweat dripping onto the phone's ripe-smelling receiver. "If you want him in the movie, you're going to have to bail him out, you know."

"I'm here to help, Kyle. We're friends now. Tell you what, I'm going to put in a call to my accountant to rearrange some funds. While we wait, how about you and I have lunch, hmm? I'm buying."

He picks me up in front of the boarded-up Caldor's and takes me to a Denny's off Exit 52, all the way in West Haven. It's mostly packed with fat white truckers eating alone. Tom orders blueberry pancakes and three scrambled eggs with a slice of American cheese on the side. A massive scab covers what looks like a popped pimple on his neck, and I keep looking at it and then the blueberries. My chicken club comes late, and I'm starving, haven't eaten anything all day. I take a huge bite, but then think of Josh and lose my appetite before swallowing. I stop eating and wait until the rumbling in my stomach subsides, along with the thought of my best friend in jail, and when it does, I eat a fry, but then think of him again and stop chewing.

"You've got to eat, Kyle." A bit of syrup is thickening on the collar of Tom's pinstriped shirt. The suit he's wearing looks like the exact one he wore the other times I've seen him, but as rich as he is, he probably owns a half-dozen of them. "It's going to be okay. We're going to work this out," he says, laying his sweaty hand on top of my clenched fist.

I pull away slowly. "Thanks, Tom. Really."

"On a positive note, I've finalized the cast for my movie." My ears perk up, and I forget for a few seconds how crappy the last week has been without Josh around. "Kyle, I'd like you to play Jacob."

I feel my mouth widening, a smile spreading across my face. He smiles back, then smothers his pancakes with more maple syrup.

...

It's the beginning of September but still sweltering out. So many people think summer ends in August, but it's not officially over till the end of September. Drenched in sweat, Tom comes in through the basement doors, probably because he doesn't want to face my mom.

"I received your voicemail, Kyle. I felt it better to come by instead of discussing this over the phone," he says, using his chubby pointer finger to lop off the thick glaze of perspiration on his forehead. I bet the reason he gets those monster zits on his neck is because of all the nasty secretions oozing out of his fat, overheated body.

"You lied to us from the first day we met you," I say. "You promised to get Josh out, and you didn't. Now he's on house arrest, and he won't even see me. I promised him because I was counting on you!" I punch at one of the shower curtains that separate my bedroom from the rest of the basement.

For the last few weeks, he's had me believing he's dying from a tumor. It's supposedly located on one side of his brain, making him walk with a limp. But he got sloppy, forgetting which leg to drag; all of a sudden it was the right leg, not the left. When I called him out on it the other day, he said I was mistaken, and then quickly reverted to the other leg. Afterward, I opened up one of the bottles of his supposedly prescribed pain meds and found over-the-counter Tylenol inside. He's been faking it the whole time, pretending that filming can't happen because he's going to die in a month or two. The

127

best part of it all is he said he's leaving me a million dollars in his will and needs me to take care of him till the end.

Mom's been convinced too. She got teary-eyed when I told her he was dying, making him food to take home. I should've known sooner something was up. His so-called accountant never came through with the money to bail out Josh, and it's been weeks since he mentioned the film. When he offered me the lead role, he gave me a consent form for Mom to sign. She was so excited. "I'm so proud of you," she said. Now, once I tell her the truth about him, everything will go back to normal.

Since Josh has been away, Tom and I have been spending a lot of time together. He's taken me to dinner then the movies almost every night, or he buys me things at the mall, mostly books, or clothes from the Gap store that just opened. We'd drive up to his house in Sherman a lot, where I'd try on my new clothes and he'd take pictures of me—sometimes in just underwear, other times in really dressy outfits like a ribbed white T-shirt, wool cargo pants and shiny black shoes. He'd say he was trying to figure out my wardrobe for the movie. He bought me all the books by Christopher Pike I didn't have, and more literary stuff like a couple Faulkner novels, and poetry collections by Anne Sexton and Arthur Rimbaud. I've read *The Bell Jar* and *Walden*, and Hemingway and Mailer, all within the last month and a half or so. He thinks most of the books I read are above my reading level, but I don't. Although I don't fully understand all of them, there are a lot of passages I like and underline, and reread later on as if they're sayings from the Bible.

"And my mother!"

"Keep your voice down, you little shit!" he says. "I haven't the foggiest idea what you're talking about, but you had better learn when to shut up."

Surprised at his sudden change in tone, I go silent.

"After all I've done for you. Can't you just be grateful? You're all the same. I'm just going to have to get through this on my own," he says, tears in his eyes. "Jesus Christ, it's so hot in here." Pulling off his sweat-soaked blazer, he reveals his gun in a holster. It catches me off guard because he usually keeps it in the glove compartment of his car.

He let me hold it once while we waited for an attendant at Mobil to fill up the gas tank in his gold Chevy Impala—*his* Impala, not his non-existent driver's personal car. The gun is a small Smith & Wesson revolver made of stainless steel that's a lot heavier than it looks. "Just about five pounds," he told me. I think its weight proves it has the power to kill. When Tom dropped it in my hands, I thought of my dumbass father almost instantly. Not sure what type of gun he'd used to rob that bank, but he had to have known what he'd been getting himself into. I think to hold a gun in your hands is to be aware of its potential implications. Wonder what weirds me out more: the weapon or the realization that the person I've been spending so much time with has turned out to be an imposter. Maybe his name isn't even Tom York, who knows.

"I don't know where you come off accusing me of fal-sifying my illness, but I can assure you, if you repeat your suspicions to your friends or family—anyone—there will be consequences." He stands and grabs his blazer, folding it over his arm. He puts his hand on my bony shoulder as he walks past me. "Good luck to you, Mr. Mason," he says.

I doubt I'll ever see him again.

...

"If I didn't have this shit on my leg, I'd be beating his ass right now," Josh says, using a pencil to scratch in between the metal bracelet and his ankle. "I knew he was a freak faggot when he had me whipping my schlong out on camera." He cackles at the memory while playing with the bracelet. "This fucking thing is so itchy!" He's on house arrest since beating up Derek and only allowed to leave for work. Herb sends Josh's probation officer Josh's work schedule every week, and if Josh isn't home within 30 minutes after his shift ends, a signal gets sent out and the police come looking for him. "We all must be pretty dumb, huh."

"Yeah," I say, feeling more disappointed than angry.

He lights a joint, blowing the smoke in my face and laughing. "He definitely loved you the most though, bro."

"I don't know. You're the one who got naked," I say, poking him in the ribs.

"Nah dude," he says, waving a hand, "it was definitely you."

Since Tom bailed I've been over at Josh's more. He seems to have lightened up about being on house arrest. Sometimes when his mom's at work, a bunch of us come by and get high with him on the front porch. He gets drug-tested once a week, but he drinks lots of water and Golden Seal to clean his piss beforehand, and it's worked so far.

Today we're hanging out alone, feeling bored till he remembers the pills the Yalie gave him. We pop five each and lie

131

on our backs in the yard, waiting for them to kick in.

"I'm glad we're hanging out again more," I say.

He scratches his balls. "Yeah bro."

"I heard Derek just got out of the hospital, but his jaw's still wired. But I don't think he'll mess with us after what you did."

"Fuck him. I hope he dies."

We both go silent for about ten minutes. Deep in thought about nothing in particular, I forget I've taken the pills, but then feel my body turning into jelly, my legs and butt getting soupy. More time passes and I become aware of my surroundings again, noticing my hand in his shorts, massaging his inner thigh, the tips of my fingers grazing his balls. Glancing at his crotch, I see he's not hard. When I look up, he's staring at me strangely. But he's drooling, appearing to be only half conscious, so even if he is a little freaked out, he probably won't remember when he's sober. I hear a car pulling up, a door slamming. His mom must be home.

The party's over.

...

Grandpa died, and the wake is on the night of his dead wife's birthday, which is probably just a weird coincidence, but it makes me wonder if there's something cosmic going on, like stars aligning so his one and only love is waiting on the other side with open arms. Our grandmother died in her forties before Max and I were born. Over 30 years have passed, and I'm almost positive he never fucked anyone after her. His sex has been bowling and the lotto and TV and Marlboro's and Little Debbie snacks dipped in Quaker Oatmeal.

Dead people are weird. Grandpa once towered over everyone like a scarecrow, but he's much smaller now. The lighting on his corpse is phosphorescent and fluorescent, purple and red. To me he doesn't look real. Max didn't either. His body was just an empty shell where my brother used to live. Lifeless meat. An old Halloween costume. His wake was on a curb, and only I got to say goodbye to the body. Mom couldn't bear to see it, so she had him cremated.

Maybe it's the acid I took earlier, but under the lights, Grandpa looks like he's breathing. I only took half a tab, which was all I had left from what Cosmo had given to me at Tunnel, so I'm not bugging out or anything. I just think it's interesting that Grandpa is alive *and* dead at the same time. It's kind of funny. He's smiling now, and it's Grandma's birthday, and maybe they're together and happy, unlike us here.

"He's still alive," I whisper to my ten-year-old sister, who's clinging to my arm like a koala bear. She runs from the room in tears, my soon-to-be-ex-stepfather telling me quietly that I'm a piece of shit, then going after her. Mark is staying with Diane. Mom says he's too young to come to the wake, which makes me laugh, considering all the shit I knew at eight.

Mom's sitting in the first row, slightly hunched over, alone. Eric dumped her for a younger chick who took her waitressing job when she got the office gig. After all the fighting and hating, I'm feeling an almost unbearable pain in my stomach when I look at her. Grandpa wasn't really a good father, but now both of her parents are dead, and it must be strange. She says it's for the best. All the hospital stays because of his emphysema, the skin cancer, the money troubles, the constant annoying visits to our house, the decades of solitude, he's better off, hopefully at peace now. Her only remaining family is what's left of her kids.

"Kyle," she says, "get up there and say goodbye to Grandpa."

On the other hand, she acts like such a victim, and can get annoying after awhile. Kneeling at the coffin, I'm thinking, fuck it, I'm not going to feel guilty for anything I've ever done; she's just as much to blame, if not more.

When she was cleaning out Grandpa's condo, she found cash hidden throughout it, which she used to pay for the funeral and leftover bills. He didn't leave anything else to us. Once in a while I check the mail to see if Tom's lawyers sent me a check for my inheritance, but it's never there.

Sometimes I read the obits in the *Connecticut Post*, but I have yet to find any mention of him dying. Any day now, I keep telling myself.

...

Where the hell is fall! This ugly green polo shirt is sticking to my sweaty torso like Saran Wrap. The nametag pinned to it says "Kyle Mason," but my identity is meaningless. No one gives a shit about me. It's like I don't exist to these people, and I'm sick of it. I never should've begged Herb for my job back. I should've gotten my GED and found something better rather than wasting time trying to be near Josh.

"You're not my girlfriend, and I'm not a fucking faggot," Josh says, "I'm done with this shit. We gotta stop hanging out, bro."

"You can't do this to me, Max!" I say, "I'm so sick of going through this with all you users!"

"Nah, hold up, you just called me Max."

Tears are in my eyes, but I'm not crying. He's not going to make me cry. But everything's boiling inside me and ready to pop. I'm furious. This is the last one. This is the ultimate disappointer. This is the final motherfucker who will fail me as a family member, friend, whatever. I loathe Josh, and I can't stand my mother again. What more is there to do or say? Nothing. God, I hate my life.

Sucking in snot, I swallow phlegm and Josh's words, then push him as hard as I can, not necessarily aiming for the metal dumpster behind him. Stunned from hitting the back of his head on it, he sort of looks up at me, eyes rolling backward. He pulls a shard of glass out of the palm of his hand, opening a gaping hole. Blood erupts from it, pouring down his arm like lava. I don't feel bad. It's his fault he's down there, bleeding like the dumbass he is. After all I've done for him! I was the only one who stayed at the hospital and tried helping him when he was in jail.

There are one or two poor drunks in the grocery store every day, turning in their empties for money, using the machine that breaks up all the beer bottles. The recycling guys are constantly emptying the dumpster later than they're supposed to, so the glass is usually overflowing onto the pavement. I almost stepped on a shard once. I should've let it stab my foot and collected workers' comp, in honor of Chuck. Maybe Josh will be the one to do that now, though if he's seriously hurt, I'll probably end up one of my father's cellmates.

Looking up at the security camera, I recall Josh smashing it with a rock a couple days ago, just for the hell of it. No one ever comes back here anyway, not even Herb. What a creepy loser that guy is. I'm tired of working for him. Plus Bridget got fired for coming to work drunk a few weeks ago, and that faggot Cosmo is getting on my nerves.

Josh is using his left hand to cover the wound on his right, blood leaking out from between his fingers like the time Derek's boy busted open his chin. If he snaps out of it, he'll probably come beat the shit out of me. I wonder if my father will come looking for me, if and when he's let out of prison. I'll be in my late twenties at least, if I live that long.

Checking the time on Josh's watch, I realize my break's almost over. There's a ten-minute limit, which is bullshit.

I'm definitely going to quit. Lighting a cigarette, I take a couple quick drags from it, flick it against the building,

go back inside.

PART TWO:
DEATH TO ORGANIZE

But suicides have a special language.
Like carpenters they want to know which tools.
They never ask why build...
– *from "Wanting to Die" by Anne Sexton*

Last winter, on January 15, 2008, a week before Heath Ledger died from a bad mix of pills and maybe coke, Brad Renfro croaked from a heroin overdose, which surprised me less because he'd been known as a white trash druggie most of his life. This isn't to say Heath had been a saint. Although his partying days hadn't been as bad as Brad's, he still ended up ruining the relationship he had with the mother of his only child. Heath, Brad and I are—or were—around the same age.

In a cab feeling desperate for something, but I don't know what. Whizzing by buildings, people and cars, I'm imagining destroying them all as easily as flicking a train of dominoes with my finger. The brick walls of this one building I'm passing are smashing into the washers and dryers in the laundromat on the first floor, obliterating the customers waiting around, soapy water washing away the blood. Other buildings are collapsing on pedestrians, bodies splattering on the pavement the way those of rats and pigeons sometimes do when the dumb pests try crossing a busy avenue and end up squashed by a car. Concrete sidewalks and potholed asphalt streets are caving in, angular pieces of rock slicing and dicing the subway riders in this hollow city.

I'm fantasizing about all this on my way to The National concert. I bought an extra ticket in case I wanted to bring someone, but I've recently realized how much I dislike my friends—advertising/banker/lawyer types—so I've decided to give it away to someone when I get there.

After the concert, I'm eating with my friend Michael at this restaurant on Bowery, and his emaciated neck is really getting to me. It looks like a chicken's neck, and it's taking all my self-control not to respond with "cluck, cluck" as he jabbers on about getting a bonus equal to only 80 percent of his annual salary rather than the full hundred. His neck shoots out the top of a collarless shirt. He looks like a farm-fresh bird in people's clothes. I don't know why we're friends.

...

"Take off your clothes," Jay orders as we walk into my apartment, where the air is so thick and sticky the walls seem to be perspiring. It's only the end of May, but the city is already boiling. He turns the air conditioner on high then pushes his damp hair behind his ears. He isn't beautiful, but he's mine, we're together, a couple. Michael says I can do much better, but what does he know.

Jay's about the same size as me: thin and toned, but he has green eyes instead of black, and buzzed blond hair rather than dark brown like mine. We look nothing alike, have nothing in common and have only been seeing each other for a couple weeks. But he sells coke, and I've been sampling his white wares quite a bit—all of last weekend and the weekend before, the following mornings of which I spent counting an infinite number of sheep.

He doesn't live in the city, and he didn't want to stay at my place when we first met off Facebook, so for our first date, he booked a suite at the Millennium Hilton. The room overlooked Ground Zero, and in the morning, after no more than an hour of beer-induced, half-conscious sleep, we held hands looking out the window at the overcast day and the big square hole in the ground filled with cranes, dozers, dumpers and excavators.

...

It's been a month since Jay and I met, and now I'm thinking I never really loved him as a person; it was more about the power in his pelvic thrust. Neither of us had ever said the L-word. He said he'd say it when he was completely sure, and I'd only be completely sure when he was, because when we were together I gauged my own feelings by those of others. Making confident decisions has never been my strong suit, and it can be really frustrating when trying to make everyday choices: subway or cab, takeout or dinner with friends, live or...well, you get the picture, and if you were looking at it then, you'd have been watching Jay coming in my asshole, but I guess we're broken up now.

I'm in Brooklyn at around 6 a.m. on a Sunday, hailing a livery cab with tinted windows, leaving one of Michael's house parties that I frequent only because his apartment's an easy place to blow lines and get drunk. He lives in one of those new luxury condos along the East River.

A car stops and I get in.

"Eleventh and A," I say.

The sketchy looking driver doesn't respond; he just drives toward the Williamsburg Bridge. Only a few hours of forced sleep are left between the LCD Soundsystem concert and me. The sun chases the cab into the darkness of Manhattan, threatening rays reflecting off the driver's rearview mirror. As we go over the bridge, I stare with bugged eyes at the *Save Domino* sign in neon red lighting, hanging on for dear life to the old sugar factory, the brightness of its fluorescent protest fading in the growing daylight. Nothing tastes sweet these days anyway.

A few stragglers from last night's parties at various clubs and lounges float clumsily along Delancey to their wormholes in brownstones and cooperative housing. On Avenue A, I see the homeless settling into cardboard apartments, their shopping carts bursting with dated magazines, empty beer bottles and Ziploc toilets full of the yellowest urine. The sweeper truck in front of us clears the debris of another debauchery-filled Saturday night, paving a clean potholed slate for the last stretch between my home and me. Each block takes an hour in my mind and less than three seconds in reality, but we eventually get there. I pay the speechless driver, thank him and get out the car.

Inside my wormhole, I'm hurrying to the closet to see if anyone's hiding in it, sticking my hand through the hanging clothes, feeling for any warm bodies. Finding none, I run into the tiny bathroom and flick on the light, thinking I might catch someone behind the translucent shower curtain, but the tub is empty. Or maybe a pervert is watching me from the fire escape, peering through the half-closed mini blinds. Perhaps he found a way to unlock the window, so right now, as I'm checking out the bathroom, he's breaking in, hiding under the bed, getting ready to attack me once I lie down. Rushing over to the window and opening the blinds, I find no one, just the cigarette-butt-ridden courtyard behind the building. I've now accepted that I'm alone, but I'll still spend my last minutes awake staring at the window, fighting to keep my eyes closed, having to remind myself over and over that no one's breaking in.

There's no food in the fridge, just half-empty bottles and jars of condiments. I find the Grey Goose in the freezer and drink the dregs of it to help me pass out and get enough rest before meeting Jay at the concert. He said he'd go. I'll admit, there've been a couple of times between the breakup and now when he said he wanted to meet but changed his mind at the last minute, accusing me of having done something crazy, but I think he was just making excuses because he's scared of his feelings for me. He sounded different when he called yesterday morning. I felt real emotion through the phone. During our conversation I heard "Never As Tired As When I'm Waking Up" by LCD Soundsystem playing in the background. That's our song. It couldn't have been a coincidence.

So what will I wear tomorrow, how will I prepare? What I really mean is, what will I wear later today. I want to look my best for Jay, show him what he's missing. And don't confuse me with some vain homo; no, think of me more as a gay Patrick Bateman, except a slightly less violent and considerably less wealthy version. I'm a serial killer who's lost his edge, a sociopath who's turned his hatred inward and mutilates his own mind rather than other people's faces or bodies.

I I I I. Do you think I say it too often? Do I talk about myself too much? Am I self-absorbed? Am I self-obsessed? What do I really want from me? All I really want is to be happy. No, I just need to fall asleep.

Checking the time on my cell phone, I see it's half past six! Where have the hours gone? My mumbling mind—hey, did you know there's a restaurant on 17th and 3rd called Mumbles? I've always wanted to go there and mumble my order to the waiter. Wouldn't that be hilarious? I bet someone else already did it though. Someone else already thought about everything you're thinking or will think.

No one is original, especially not me, and neither is the overpowering daylight pouring into the apartment. I turn on my cheap air conditioner; it softens the noises coming from the apartments of my neighbors, who are up and ready to take on a new day before I'm able to sleep off the last one. Why hasn't Jay called yet to confirm? I don't know if I can fall asleep before he and I decide on a time and place to meet. Should we meet here, in my wormhole? Would it be awkward? It's fucking 6:45 now. What am I going to do? I'm just going to call him. Should I call him? I'm not even tired anymore; I slept late Friday night, anyway, and I've technically been sleeping since I'm lying in bed with my eyes closed. I feel fine. He's probably waiting for me to call. I know, I'll call him and offer to take him out for dinner and drinks before the concert. Yeah, that's it. That's what I'll do.

"Hey Jay, listen, I know I sound retarded. Long night. I'm just a little tired and not feeling well. Call me. Let me take you out for a drink before the concert tonight."

Five minutes pass and no response. Okay, maybe he's a little unsure. Should I just go to his place like I did the other times he didn't answer the phone?

"Hey Jay, I hope you're still up for going to the concert with me. Anyway, let me know what you're doing for the rest of the day. I could totally use a good meal, especially after getting hardly any sleep!"

Another five minutes pass, and I still don't hear from him. What the fuck? We're supposed to meet today. He won't even call me back? Who does he think he is?

"Jay, this is fucking ridiculous. You're ignoring me because you can't handle your emotions? Okay, maybe I've been a little crazy. But how long have we been seeing each other? And you know I hate being ignored. Call me back. Bye."

Ten minutes go by. I may as well have porn on because I can hear my next-door neighbor, this massive black dude, pounding some slut on the other side of the thin wall that separates our apartments. Ah! I can't wait around anymore! I know Jay's home. I'm going over there.

Sitting up, I feel my phone vibrating on the bed—a text from Jay! I open the message, read the one-word text in all caps: PSYCHO. My thoughts immediately following his foul response are a bunch of jigsaw puzzle pieces that don't fit together. But using force, I connect them until they form a discernible decision in my mind: razorblade.

"Take off or I'm calling the cops!" he yells through the thin backdoor to his apartment. If I slam my body against it, I bet I'd be able to break it down.

"Let me in!" I shout back, not caring if I disturb the neighbors. "I just want to talk. Please! I came all the way here."

At about eight this morning I went to Duane Reade on 14th and 1st to steal some waterproof bandages—I'd blown all my cash on ski, and I don't get paid for another week and a half. After removing and discarding the blood-soaked Band-

Aids I'd been wearing, I rinsed my wounds with peroxide then delicately applied antibiotic ointment and the more suitable coverings. Taking a shower was like playing a watersport; I had to wash my body while trying not to get my wrists wet.

As satisfied with my look as I could've been with fresh flesh wounds and no sleep, I made the 9:23 a.m. train on the New Haven line.

...

The rusty razorblade was still in the utensil drawer underneath a stack of imitation stainless steel forks from Ikea. Jay used it to cut out the old painted-over light switches when I'd moved into this wormhole.

He was right about me being crazy. But it was his fault. It was their fault. I hated them all, and I hated the dimmers he'd installed. Smacked the veins in my arms. *I hated myself. I hated myself. I hated myself and I wanted to die—declarations similar to the lyrics in a song by Cat Power, yes, but it was also the way I was feeling, the way I was cutting into my wrists.* No, not cutting. Chopping.

After making countless potholes in my skin, I raced to the bathtub, turned on the faucet and got in, my blood quickly turning the transparent water into a cloudy red color just like the cliché suicide scenes in countless movies. Allowed the faucet to run a minute or two before turning it off. The hemorrhaging slowed then stopped.

"Fuck," I said to myself because the blade was over on the bed, so I couldn't finish myself off.

Some of the thick scabs are falling off by themselves, and the rest I've been picking with dirty untrimmed fingernails. I'm dreading the lumpy scars—they'll be constant reminders of what I did to myself, every time I unlock a door, smear pomade in the palm of my hand or button a shirt. Should've gotten stitches.

...

Belts on my scarred wrists are restricting my movements. Drugs weigh down my head. The sleepy policewoman at the door, the disapproving nurse, Michael looking tired and irritated, all of it sucks, but nothing sucks worse than the burning, intrusive sensation of this thin rubber tube shoved inside the hole of my cock. I haven't regained consciousness because I want to live; I just have to take a piss.

"I have to pee," I say, weakly lifting the loose-fitting hospital gown, finding tubing attached to my limp dick.

"So pee," Michael says. He's sitting next to the medical bed, a crinkled newspaper in his lap.

"What happened?"

"I had no choice but to call an ambulance. You showed up intoxicated out of your mind this morning and then locked yourself in the bathroom for hours. I couldn't have you dying in my apartment."

"I wasn't dying."

"You were hostile. And the cops came and wanted to arrest you...I spent the last couple hours convincing them not to."

Brad Renfro's fatal overdose comes to mind; his girlfriend discovered the body. Michael found mine, but it's not the same, unfortunately. I try pushing out the piss. At first the maneuver just forces the tubing deeper inside, the burning making me wince.

"I wasn't this time," I say. "I mean, I didn't."

He doesn't respond as the room begins to spin. To fight off the nausea, I'm keeping my eyes closed, but it's not helping.

The nurse comes back in the room. "The hospital psychiatrist will be here in a few minutes for your psych eval," she says.

"How long do I have to be here?" I ask, my head swaying like a rocking dinghy in choppy waters.

"Forty-eight hours," she says, replacing the drip.

"Two days!"

The cop peers in the room.

"Policy for suicide attempts," the nurse says.

"But I didn't try to kill myself! I was just drunk and took too many pills."

Giving me a cold look, she then glances at Michael. "Speak with the doctor," she says.

In the meantime, I try pissing again, this time successfully, but I can't get it all out. The catheter's a real bitch; it feels as if I'm trying to piss after blowing a load. I check the time on Michael's watch to get my mind off the uncomfortable feeling. It's 8 a.m. He comes over and squeezes my shoulder, then returns to the chair next to the bed and reopens the *New York Post*.

The psychiatrist will be in soon. I have to collect my thoughts, appear sane and straight, or else I'll be sitting in this hellhole for nearly half a week. I really will kill myself then.

The psychiatrist practically crawls in on his hands and knees, has obviously been working all night. "And how are we feeling?" he asks, sighing heavily.

"Fine. A little hungover."

"Do you want to tell me what you were doing with the pills, the...Xanax?" he says, reading from his little chart.

"I have a prescription for them."

He doesn't look up as he scratches around the outside of his left nostril. "And what was causing the anxiety last night?"

"I don't know. Nothing," I say even-toned, not wanting to tell him the truth. "I shouldn't have taken the pills with the booze, but I was definitely not trying to commit suicide."

The doctor approves my release though the pills haven't worn off. The nurse removes the rubber straw in my cock, which is a relief, but I still have to resist my head's desire to roll around. By the time Michael drops me home I'm feeling much better. It's such a hot and muggy morning, but I left the air conditioner on all night.

...

Julia gazes out the window onto 87th Street on a cool day. Reflections of pedestrians in her circular eyeglasses are covering her eyes. I'm seeing short, fat silhouettes whizzing by the lenses, tall slender forms taking their time and little dots hopping. Is she even listening? I suppose her unresponsiveness could be her way of absorbing everything I've been saying.

She's wearing a white one-piece outfit, the top part collared with buttons like a dress shirt, the bottom half extending past her knees like a skirt. It's fun! It's summery! It goes well with her short auburn hair and vintage eyeglasses. What a sophisticated look for an older woman.

But these psychoanalysts kill me! Their outfits and home offices and windows and streets. These little ladies. What a job. I should study to become a New York City psychoanalyst. All I'd have to do is sit in my Upper East Side co-op listening to people whine about their miserable lives. Then I'd never feel bad about my own, and when I got bored or sick of listening, I'd stare at the people walking down the street—my chair *right* next to the window—my patient wondering the whole time if I was even listening. I'd be getting paid to do absolutely nothing other than wasting a few hours of my day. I wouldn't have to work at the ad agency anymore, and in between appointments I'd blow straight guys who'd respond to ads I'd post on Craigslist every morning.

"Why did you come here today, Kyle?" she asks, eyeing me dead-on—a striking variation from the brick wall I was just talking to.

Julia's a "therapist to the stars," at least that's what Michael was telling me after setting up the appointment. The only reason I agreed to go was because I felt like I owed him for the whole hospital ordeal.

She's waiting patiently for an answer to the question, mouth frozen, hands folded on a stiff lap. When was the last time someone fucked her good? Probably never.

I'd love to grab that umbrella leaning against the wall to her left and jam it between her legs, shove it in her cunt and pierce it through her back, opening it behind her, loosening her up.

...

Jay walks into my wormhole looking like a bloated sausage. He sure did gain weight this past month. Affecting an expression of pity, he closes the front door then comes to where I'm lying on the bed, black MacBook in my lap, Netflix on the screen. I keep quiet as he climbs over me and gets under the covers. We lie together like a couple sardines. Then we make moves, and I quickly realize how much I hate him now. His breath smells like a dump truck, and his kisses are slimy. Shoving my hand down his pants, I feel his grotesquely oversized cock and small disproportionate balls. You're disgusting, I say to him in my head. Get off me.

"You should go," I say out loud.

His eyes tear up—a physical response to him assuming guilt as if any of this had anything to do with him. Bet Michael the Chicken messaged Jay on Facebook and told him what had happened. They need to mind their own business.

"Why? I thought you'd be happy to see me?" he asks.

"Now's not a good time," I say, turning on my side. "I have work tomorrow. I shouldn't have said it was cool for you to come."

He agrees to leave on the stipulation that I let him come back on Friday with an eight-ball of coke to get me high, then take me to Kmart on Astor Place to buy random cheap shit—a pastime with him I once thought was funny and romantic but which I now find dumb and trashy.

The next morning, I'm staring at a computer monitor, unblinkingly. A blank Word document is covering the screen like a starched white bed sheet, a restless cursor with a mind of its own refuting the comparison, going in and out of visibility with irritating quickness like a taunting adolescent. Should call the IT help desk and get a new mouse, but I don't care enough.

My arms rest on a sickly gray plastic desktop that encompasses three sides of the cubicle in which I'm sitting. There are no picture frames or green plants to offset the dust balls or crusty stains from last week's lunches, just unorganized piles of incomplete copywriting assignments, a folder holder filled with dated magazines and an HR orientation package I never opened, and two newspaper clippings about the overdoses of Brad Renfro and Heath Ledger pinned to an otherwise unused corkboard.

Desk phone rings. My micromanaging boss Deana is in the lobby. She usually works out of the Boston office, but she's in New York this week. She's a decent human being, I guess, but as with any authority figure that's ever been in my life, I appreciate a huge amount of space between her and me. Fairly certain that since her last visit to New York her affection toward me has morphed into an unnatural motherly concern—don't think she believed me when I tried explaining the big bandages on my wrists. *Was picking up a tray of wine glasses to serve friends at a cocktail party when the tray suddenly slipped from my hands, wine glasses smashing against the kitchen counter, shards of glass cutting up my inner arms.*

She's said on more than one occasion that she thinks her

adolescent son is gay, hence why she's been so keen on me for as long I've been working here, that is until the whole bandage mishap. Oh well.

...

Medicated days are bullshit escapes. I'm living them at the moment, these dizzy daydreams filled with muted emotions; I have been treated. I'm definitely not cured, but then again it's only been two weeks since I began popping more pills. Xanax per usual. But now Zoloft, too. And Lamictal with side effects such as mouth sores, fatigue and zombie brain. My usual self has been abbreviated and I don't like it; I've replaced suicide with sertraline, cocaine lines with lamotrigine. When I'm not in a relationship, I love getting fucked by multiple guys and doing blow on a regular basis, but since I've had my mind prescribed, it's less alluring, and for the most part, unsatisfying.

"Don't you remember?" my mother asks, and no, I don't. She reverses out of a parking space near the mall entrance where she says she once found me dressed in dirty clothes, sitting drunk on the ground and cutting myself with a razorblade before a small audience of "strange teens." My visit to Connecticut has been an amnesiac's trip down memory lane, probably because I'm still getting used to my new set of meds and recovering from the overdose—which she knows nothing about.

The dinner she makes is delicious, but the conversation is dull, as it's been for years now. She takes a sip of water and clears her throat, and when I do the same thing a couple minutes later, I notice the sound of the action is identical. It's like we're the same person, if only in this simple way.

While a pie bakes in the oven, she sits on the couch watching *Law & Order*, my second stepfather puffs on a cigarette blowing smoke up the fireplace, and I walk down the hallway inspecting photos on the walls: young me, medium me, younger half-siblings I never see, dead older brother— none of us saying much of anything.

I have a hookup waiting for me when I get back home, a guy I used to see before dating Jay. The guy fucks me.

"I'm seeing someone," he confesses while dressing.

"Oh yeah?"

"Yeah, it's funny. I mean, we've been going together for three weeks now, and we haven't done *anything*." He pulls on his T-shirt, zips up his jeans.

"Nothing?"

"Nope, he's a really nice guy."

"Nice," I say, making my way into the bathroom to wipe off the rest of the come on me that I failed to eat. I close the bathroom door.

"I'm seeing someone," I say to myself in the mirror.

"Oh yeah?" my mirror-self asks.

"Yeah, it's funny. We just barebacked, and I didn't feel *anything*."

"Nothing?"

"Nope," I say, "I mean, I didn't even come, but he's a really nice guy."

"Nice."

Coming back out, I see the guy's left without saying goodbye. When I'm diluted with daily medication, my heart's covered in an opaque sheet, and I feel nothing.

...

I'm with Michael at Regal Cinemas in Union Square, reading an article about Heath Ledger, waiting for *The Dark Knight* to begin. We're sitting in the back row, getting drunk off Jack and Diet Cokes, paying no attention to each other. He's busy on his work Blackberry; my nose is in the *New York Post*. Apparently, Heath's 20-million-dollar fortune will go to his daughter, Matilda Rose. He never updated his will after she'd been born, so there was much discourse over whether his parents and three sisters would be awarded all his earnings or if the money should go to his kid. Guess he never thought to change it 'cause he didn't think he'd be dying so early in life. Lesson learned: always be prepared for your worst self. Which is why I've written out my will in a copy of *The Complete Poems: Anne Sexton*.

The Dark Night grossed 155.4 million dollars opening weekend. That's more than 15 billion pennies. I'm distracted by a daydream about me drowning in the Atlantic Ocean during a tsunami, skyscraper-tall waves made of billions of pennies substituting for the saltwater kind. Each penny was made in 1980, the year my brother was born. We collected them when we were younger. I used to save the 1982 ones; he'd do the same for his birth year. When he died, I threw out all of mine. Not sure where his are.

When Heath comes on screen for the first time, everyone applauds and I get a hard-on. It's not sexual, but it's...something. Better than the other night. I text myself lines from the movie that I find meaningful, lines like *the night is darkest just before the dawn.*

"What are you doing, weirdo?" Michael asks, chuckling.

"Drown yourself," I say.

I'll later learn some guy named Thomas Fuller originated the saying in the 1800s.

"You already know about Heath, but I also have this weird obsession with Brad Renfro," I say.

"He's a musician?" Julia asks, adjusting her eyeglasses.

"Actor. You know, it's funny; my favorite movie when I was thirteen or so was *The Client*. That was his first movie. The single mom in the film reminded me of my mother. She was a waitress then, too. And my brother was Brad, and I was the younger brother he took care of."

She turns her head, does that looking-out-the-window thing she likes to do. *God*, I should've just gone to the gym with Michael.

"And Susan Sarandon played the surrogate mother to Brad's character in the movie. Now that I think back on it, she reminds me of my friend's stepmother; she was always cooler about things when I was a kid."

She still doesn't respond. I've caught on to her plan. Normally, when the patient speaks, the therapist responds with the standard "and how did/does that make you feel?" Ms. Psychoanalyst here doesn't perform as predicted. She prefers to say nothing. And the silence is so uncomfortable for the patient—me in this case—that he has no other choice but to babble on. What I expect when I pay some supposed crazy person-expert 90 bucks a visit is for her to tell me how to get my head on straight.

"You know what, this is my last session," I say impulsively. She meets my proclamation with wide eyes—the most extraordinary expression I've seen on her face yet. Uncrossing her legs, she brings her knees tightly together. Her leather-soled heels hit the hardwood floor, and it makes me think of tap dancing.

A rainstorm rages outside, yet again. It's been like this all week, and I'm sick of it. Globs of water punch the infamous window. I didn't bring an umbrella. As I stand, the chair pushes back, slamming the wall behind me. It would seem to the naked eye I did this to be dramatic, but it was accidental.

"Kyle, you're not ready to stop. It's highly inadvisable," she says, removing her eyeglasses. "If you're uncomfortable with me, I can refer you to a couple different colleagues of mine, but you shouldn't stop going. You need to be seen at least once a week until—"

"Till what?"

Her lips quiver slightly. "Until you're stable," she says. Actually, she breathes it. It flows out of her mouth, like a mother gently pushing her boy onto the bus for his first day of kindergarten. "And knowing yourself will only make you a happier person."

"Thanks for your time," I say, handing her the cash.

Reaching the exit, I hesitate in the doorway. The noise of thunder beating the sky makes me pause—possibly reconsider? I mean, stability would be nice. A small part of me wants it...

Nah.

"Should've grabbed her umbrella," I say to myself, walking into the rain.

...

A nightmare lying on my desk, a coiled snake, a scab from this morning: the tie is long and thin, made of Irish wool, cut by hand in Long Island City, dried come encrusted on it with a sprinkle of cigarette ash. My brain is a dehydrated prune, making every part of my egg-shaped head pulsate with pain, and I need a haircut. I always look older when I haven't been to the barber, especially when waking up. I'm getting old. But I should've thought about that before. An overstuffed schnoz leads to a packed sinus cavity, a self-inflicted avalanche. I'm a snow beast.

But I wasn't alone. The first one left around two, those pebbly white lines up our noses, his slimy white business down my throat. His cock traced the crack of my ass, then penetrated me. He could've been anyone, his come interchangeable with any other nobody's, as if I were lying on my back, blindfolded, throwing knives in the air above me.

I haven't eaten or left my wormhole in over 18 hours. Last night my other self lay on the edge of the bed, watching the actual me by the couch, looking as if he were judging the scene, turning his head in disgust and disappointment. But the sucking made him curious, the fucking made him wonder, and he crawled to where I was on my knees slobbering, eyes watering, and then on my back, face wincing, asshole prolapsing.

The first one said he wanted to stay. He wanted to fall asleep in my squeaky bed, cover himself in my dirty sheets, except his boyfriend was waiting. The boyfriend allowed him the time with me as long as he wasn't alone in the morning. The first one left.

Powdery remnants from four empty baggies littered the coffee table. Blue Moon beer bottles everywhere. A drinking glass filled with polluted water and two-cigarette-packs worth of extinguished butts. The bright screen on my laptop beat down on me like a stage light, an imaginary audience anticipating whom I'd select as my next visitor. But it wasn't that easy. There was posting and reading and responding and sending and waiting and deleting, deleting, deleting to do. And I was doing it, searching the digital city, and wetting my parched throat with the last few drops of alcohol, and sniffing ivory-colored crumbs.

The second one lived in Breezy Point, close to Fort Tilden, nowhere near the East Village. But he had a car. Even though it was 6 a.m. by the time I found him, he said he'd drive and I agreed to wait. Thirty minutes later the bell rang. I was already in bed, my fingers putting pressure under my eyes, a futile attempt to relieve the throbbing. Throwing on a red T-shirt that said "Dandy" in big white letters across the front of it, I hit the button and let him in.

The second one was shorter than me, a could-be-clean-cut Caucasian who dressed otherwise. His dingy baggy khakis, extra-large navy blue T-shirt and soiled Nikes. His buzzed black hair, big green eyes, nice round face and several tattoos drawn on olive skin. I loved his deep voice and brusquely masculine mannerisms, I liked that the rest of him was adequately sized. Men as women christened my computer. He made me watch them in between snorts off his cock.

Before either of us knew it, the time had passed, the treats he brought finished. But he knew someone to text. He used to work in the business, and he had numbers. We stared at our phones, nothing happening. A tiny red light flashing. Spam email. Little sister. Michael requesting my presence at a brunch. It wasn't what we wanted.

His agitation grew as his body wilted. He wanted none of it. Don't touch him. He didn't want to finish. Next time he'll listen to his bed when it's calling his name. No joy rides or ski lifts. Just a quiet room with closed windows and cool air blowing from a purring machine. He had to leave, because the sooner he did, the quicker what he'd done with me had never happened. He left.

Sticky residue remaining from my saliva-slick fingers sopping up talcum-like scraps. A spent bottle of Polish vodka. Three Parliaments mounted on a hardened wad of chewing gum attached to the bottom shelf of the bookcase. Passable pre-op trannies getting head in a video playing on a loop. I was frightened of the time, unwilling to confirm the hour.

But I shouldn't have been so hard on myself, so unwilling to accept that they'd gone, the sun was piercing the blinds, I needed to eat something and I'd been awake more than 24 hours. What a life, I thought. What a pointless existence: a weekly weekend venture into sexual depravity and self-destructive indulgence. I was alone.

I had to catch up on my sleep, if possible. I couldn't have another incident like when Jay and I had broken up. But at that point my heart was still beating as if it were a drum in a marching band, my mind running in circles like a hamster in one of those plastic balls, the rodent in my brain soldiering on, the occasional pellet-shaped shit ejecting from its asshole, involuntarily. Coming down, I believed my life was nothing but feces, and I was looking for a way to defecate it out. Via knife would've left scars if I survived, which take months to fade. The pill route had gone awry the last time. There had to be another way. Hanging? I searched the smooth ceiling, found nowhere from which to dangle indefinitely.

But the idea of strangulation stuck in my mind. Coincidentally, I'd only recently learned that when one is strangled to death, it's usually because the flow of blood is cut off from the brain rather than oxygen from the lungs. I pondered which tools I had lying around the apartment. Belt? Nope, I never wear them, the ones I own packed away in the back of the closet. Rope? Didn't have any. Using electrical wire was a possibility, although I'd have to unplug a few electronics. Too much of a project.

Sorting through the top drawer of the dresser, I found the winning instrument: a gray wool tie from J.Crew. Lying on my back on the bed, I wrapped the fabric around my neck and knotted it once. Holding one end with one hand and the other with the other, I was able to tighten the grip of the tie. I felt around for an artery carrying blood to the brain, and believing I'd found it, focused on constricting that area of the neck as much as possible. Die, coke-whore. Die, pussy. Die, faggot.

I became lightheaded. Opening my eyes, I noticed the sun had gotten brighter, the dove-colored paint on the walls had taken on a whiter hue, and I felt as if I were about to pass out. But I didn't. I was wide-awake, and instead of dying, I got to thinking about the night: those anonymous first and second cocks, the small mountain of cocaine, and the loads of come.

Stimulating memories of risky debaucheries halted my masochistic mission; rather than killing me, the asphyxiation made me unbearably horny. Keeping the tie as taut as possible with one hand, I freed the other, using it to satiate myself to completion. After wiping the results off my body, I tossed the tie on the desk and passed out, satisfied.

Too bad I'm not going to Julia anymore. Would've loved

to see her lack of reaction when I told her about this.

...

Messaged Jay on Facebook.

Dear Jay,

Thank you for calling. Hearing your voice reminded me of the fun phase, and when we fell in something we never acknowledged. It also reminded me of your kitchen counter and what we made on it; we realized that everything delicious isn't edible.

During the conversation, you reminisced about the hours we'd wasted on cartoon marathons and my mouth during those uncut-coke hangovers. I miss those things too.

But since you've been gone, I've been busy toiling, slobbering and snorting away the days. My needs have evolved. I've cocooned myself and only know how to be alone now.

Your voice took me back—a warm fuzziness ran through me, through me *and then returned to the past. I'm sorry to have answered the phone and lifted your hopes. I know you're struggling with living, too, looking for a reason in me. But to me, now, you're just an old photo album that I dusted off, opened, perused and closed again.*

Good luck,
Kyle

Jay messaged me on Facebook, then removed me from his list of friends.

Go fuck urself psycho.

...

Clock on my phone says 11:11 a.m. as I set the alarm to snooze again. Dropping the phone on the floor, I turn on my side. Before closing my eyes for the third time, I glance at the uncovered window. I don't get what all the fuss has been about. Everyone's been swearing there's going to be another big storm today, but as far as I can see, there's nothing going on out there except for a light drizzle.

Deanna calls a few minutes later, waking me up for good. She wants to know if I'll be coming into the office today. She doesn't ask in that demanding-boss tone; she's more concerned with how I'm doing, if I'm feeling better. I tell her yes, I'll be in shortly, blaming my slow start on the crappy weather.

Door to the bathroom opens, and a European-looking guy appears. He has a thick, greasy head of hair. He comes and sits on the edge of my bed, putting on a worn pair of black and electric blue, medium-top Nikes. "Later bud," he says, rubbing my head with his knuckles, then walking out. Trying to remember how we met, but the hangover is making it difficult.

At the deli downstairs from my office in Tribeca, I'm having trouble deciding what to eat for breakfast. I'm just going to buy it all: an everything bagel toasted with scallion cream cheese, a single serving of raisin bran cereal, assorted sliced fruit, a whole orange, Tropicana orange juice—not

173

from concentrate and with some pulp—and a bacon, egg and cheese with salt, pepper, ketchup. Oh, and a blueberry muffin toasted with butter. I pay for the food with my new credit card from Citi.

In my somber cubicle, I'm staring at the smorgasbord of food before me and decide I'm not hungry. Text comes in on my cell phone from a number I don't recognize. *Wanna do it again man?* I must've hooked up with this person, although not sure who it is right off the bat.

I take a cab from Tribeca back to the East Village where the dude lives. I vaguely remember him and being in his apartment. He has a nice face and toned torso, thin legs and an average cock that I suck while he jerks me off. Without warning he comes in my mouth. Swallowing it, I come too, dress quickly and leave without saying goodbye.

Outside his apartment, I hail a cab and call my mother. We talk about superficial things, the weather and how she loves the Didion novel I bought her for her birthday. The cab driver brings me back to Tribeca.

In the office again, I'm staring out the window. The rain is coming down harder. Deciding I'll use it as an excuse to leave early, I call Deanna, telling her I'm heading out for the day. "Are you okay?" she asks. "Go home and get there safe!"

The pouring rain is a translucent veil draped over Tribeca and Soho. Luckily, the office manager at work had an extra umbrella. Stopping at Angelika on Broadway and Mercer, I buy a single ticket to *What We Do Is Secret*, a film about Darby Crash, lead singer of The Germs. Watching the film, I eat chocolate-covered peanut M&M's and drink a Diet Coke. My snacks are the only enjoyable part of the movie.

Exiting the theater I check my iPhone; no one's texted or called. I walk uptown to Strand, a used bookstore in Union Square. I buy two books by Aldous Huxley, *Brave New World* and *Those Barren Leaves*, which were printed in 1925 and falling apart. Michael sends me a text, inviting me to dinner. I decline.

Stopping at a gourmet grocery store on First Avenue, I'm trying to buy just vegetables, but the bill is less than three bucks, and the store has a credit card minimum of five dollars, so I'm forced to grab a bag of Green Mountain tortilla chips and salsa to meet the mark.

In the lobby of my apartment building, I check the mailbox. In it is the latest issue of *Interview*, which I'll add to the ever-growing stack of magazines I'll never read. There's also an envelope containing two tickets to a concert by Bright Eyes, one of which I'll probably end up tossing in the trash or selling on Craigslist.

Inside my wormhole, I rest my packages on the kitchen counter, then text my dealer.

...

I've posted an ad on Craigslist that says I'm looking to blow a straight guy. One dude sends me two pictures, both of which he's taken of himself in front of a bathroom mirror. His right arm is curled upward like a bodybuilder does when showing off his muscles, except this guy's arms are more lean and toned than big and bulky. A stiff Yankees cap, turned just slightly to the left, sits snugly on his head. His olive skin and black eyebrows make him look Mediterranean, perhaps Italian or Portuguese. He says he needs thirty minutes to shower and that he'll text me when he's on his way.

In the meantime, I continue exploring my options. Another guy responds to my ad, one who looks much more like the proverbial frat-boy I usually prefer to blow, at least from the waist down: white, tall and solid with a big cock. God, I want him, wish I could see his face. We email back and forth dirty words that describe what I'm going to do to him and how he wants it. He asks that I be wearing nothing but boxer briefs and long black dress socks when I open the door to him. He says he's going to arrive with a mask on his face; he works at an investment bank, so he needs to be discreet.

I'm just about to send him my address when I receive a text from the first applicant; he's in the lobby. Frantic, I consider telling him to go away so I can have the second guy over, but online tricks are so flaky I don't want to take the chance of sending the first one home and then having the other cancel. Contemplating the situation further, I decide that I'll blow the first guy quickly and then have the second guy over afterward for a much longer suck session. I email the second guy my address along with explicit instructions for him to arrive in thirty minutes or more, definitely no earlier. That should be enough time for me to hookup with the first guy and rinse out my mouth.

I text my first guest the buzzer code and wormhole number. After about five more minutes my doorbell rings. My heart quivers a little; I always feel a slight rush when they first arrive. I'm numb to it now that I've been hooking up for however many months—okay, years—but I still feel a little something.

I open the door and he walks into my dimly lit foyer, squinting through the low-key lighting to check me out. I've left on barely any lights, not because I don't look like my picture, but because the darkness makes me more confident during the initial meet-and-greet. My bedroom's much brighter, and there we both get a good look at each other; I can tell he's pleased.

As he advances toward me while unzipping his slightly baggy jeans, we make brief eye contact and share a mild, mutually uncomfortable giggle. That's the only other form of communication we've had since saying hello. He's taller than he appeared in his pictures, and while he is thin, his shoulders are broader and his muscles more pronounced than I anticipated. The boxers he wears are so white and crisp they must be either brand new or freshly bleached and ironed, especially when compared with the dingy white T-shirt he has on.

When he smiles, I notice a slight crook in the alignment of his lower teeth, but his masculine, almost boyish face, dark olive skin and sexy body make up for the imperfection. Actually, the orthodontic error makes him that much more desirable.

After only a few minutes of me sucking his perfectly shaped cock, he pulls me up and makes me kiss him. I never kiss men I have sex with anymore and normally would resist, but this time I don't. We make our way onto the bed and finish what we were doing in the style of long-acquainted lovers. Suddenly, it's not just about satisfying our primal needs but more about filling our souls' lonely voids, which is the real reason why gay men have promiscuous sex anyway. At least that's why I do.

Finished, we discuss some of the hundreds of books I keep on my bookshelves. He says he's fond of Fante's works. He tells me his name as he walks out, but I won't make an effort to remember it 'cause it doesn't matter; he's supposed to be straight, so I doubt I'll see him again.

A few minutes after he's gone, he sends me a text: *Hey bro, I hate to ruin the thrill of anonymous sex, but after seeing you for a second time, I'm really intrigued and would be awesome to take you on an actual date.*

Remembering he's the one who slept over the night before the rainstorm, I smile, beam and then respond with, "No thanks."

A few minutes later, I'm answering the door again, and without hesitation, inviting the young banker into my wormhole. He wears over his head a black dust bag made of thick cotton, and has on a heavily worn pair of Sperry Topsider boat shoes, which are camel-colored and have white rubber soles. Paired with Kelly green shorts and a dingy white polo shirt over a chiseled chest, he looks like a Ralph Lauren model—minus the black bag on his head.

I bet he wasn't wearing the bag when he entered the building. To any of my neighbors who were coming and going as he was arriving, I'm sure he looked just like them or even better. But he probably wasn't paying attention to passersby because if he didn't acknowledge them then maybe they wouldn't notice him or wonder what he was doing. The black dust bag was most likely neatly folded and stuffed into the back pocket of his shorts like a handkerchief. To an onlooker it may have appeared as if he were trying to give his preppy style a hipster twist, a little East Village edge, even though he lives in Gramercy Park.

Neither of us speaks as I lead him to the bed. His hairy leg jerks back as it brushes against the glass top of the coffee table.

"You don't mind if I do a line, do you?" I ask, sniffling.

He shakes his head. He doesn't give a shit. He just wants a blowjob.

Doing a line off a nearby surface then quickly returning to where he's standing, I stuff a trembling hand down his shorts and pull out his thick cock. He forcefully brings me to my knees so I can get to work. I do a clumsy job, but I can tell it feels amazing to him.

After he comes, he starts hyperventilating in the dust bag, as if feelings of guilt and shame are invading his nervous system. Ripping it off, he rushes out in silence; nevertheless, I get a glimpse of his neatly groomed short dark hair, blue eyes, full lips and sharp cheekbones, and defined jaw line on a beautiful face. I wish he looked at me before leaving.

...

Some guy named Sean messaged me on Facebook.

Sean:

Hey kyle this is sean im kinda related sorta ur father is married to my mother ur father would like to talk to u if it ok can u message me bak hes been trying to get ahold of u pls message me bak thanks sean

Me:

My father is in prison, so I don't know how he's married to your mother. Either way, I have no interest in communicating with him. Tell him to leave me alone. Thanks, K.

Sean:

hes out hes at my house at nobel av hes been out now for 2 weeeks

Me:

I do not wish to communicate with him. Tell him I said good luck and do not contact me again.

Sean:

ok sry just did wut he asked he asked if i could locate u so i did but ill make sure he gets the message he in a halfway house so ill let him no

Me:

No worries. Thanks for reaching out.

...

I'm usually tending to an imaginary itch when I scratch my face, believing another outbreak is on the way. So I slather on 25-dollar cream, pop a couple antiviral horse pills and cross my fingers.

This all could've been avoided. This virus is something new. This is not a family inheritance. This is a sexual contraction. This is a fat kid who's been eating too much cake. This is the result of rubbing too many cocks on my face. Michael, that arrogant asshole, is always telling me how surprised he is I don't have any diseases, considering my frequently irresponsible sex life. Clearly, he can spare the astonishment, but I won't be telling him that.

I'm pretty sure which dude gave it to me. He's my favorite: massive, thick, rough, straight. The online photo he uses is one of him posing with an award he won at a golf tournament. He was thinner then. He's kind of fat now. But his cock is too, so the chunk's never bothered me.

He was my first time being digitally recorded. My first time drinking piss. My first time bare-backing. I can't remember how many times we'd be up at eleven in the morning, on our umpteenth line and fifth or sixth molly, watching countless videos he'd made of himself fucking random girls, none of whom had been aware of the camera.

When I told myself I was done partying for awhile, when I forced myself to stay in on a Friday night—*don't check the sketchy email, don't go to Michael's party, don't call "the guy" and blow rent money*—that was when my favorite texted. Sensing my apprehension, he offered to bring the avalanche to me, and I agreed.

That night the tip of his cock was red, bumpy and crusty, which I chalked up to him jerking off too much—an idiotic assumption from my high and horny self. I knew something was off, that his cock and my mouth had company. I knew I'd wake up one day with sore-riddled lips, and swollen and tender gums, followed by scars and more sores. And I'd have to apply 25-dollar cream and swallow antiviral horse pills, and deal with paranoia about the next outbreak, and embarrassment from being seen in public when it finally came. They'd all know. They'd all see. They'd think *there's that faggot cocksucker, just another faggot cocksucker*. But maybe it's all in my head. I can hardly tell the difference anymore.

At least I'll have the memory of my favorite hookup—the consequence of an animalistic, insatiable lust for the fantasy of a dead brother and murderous father whose faces I can't remember without looking at their photos—literally written all over my face for

the rest of my life.

Christopher Stoddard is the author of the
book, *White, Christian* (Spuyten Duyvil/Triton, 2010).
He lives in Brooklyn. Visit antichrispress.com.